BARBARA PITCAIRN

BARBARA PITCAIRN

Inga Dunbar

Chivers Press • Thorndike Press
Bath, England   Thorndike, Maine USA

This Large Print edition is published by Chivers Press, England, and by Thorndike Press, USA.

Published in 2000 in the U.K. by arrangement with Piatkus.

Published in 2000 in the U.S. by arrangement with Judith Murdock, Agent.

U.K. Hardcover ISBN 0–7540–4160–3 (Chivers Large Print)
U.K. Softcover   ISBN 0–7540–4161–1 (Camden Large Print)
U.S. Softcover   ISBN 0–7862–2565–3 (General Series Edition)

The text of this Large Print edition is unabridged.
Other aspects of the book may vary from the original edition.

Set in 16 pt. New Times Roman.

Printed in Great Britain on acid-free paper.

British Library Cataloguing in Publication Data available

Library of Congress Cataloging-in-Publication Data

Dunbar, Inga.
    Barbara Pitcairn / Inga Dunbar.
        p.   cm.
    ISBN 0–7862–2565–3 (lg. print : sc : alk. paper)
    1. Large type books.   I. Title.
    PR6054.U4579 B37   2000
    823'.92—dc21   00–028645

PROLOGUE

Far, far to the north, at the end of the world, the icebergs cracked and broke. Thunderous seas carried their icy splinters south past the towering stacks, through the fearsome clefts in the cliffs, to roar and boom up the long caverns around the islands of Shetland.

The two white seals on their bed of pearls awoke in the shock of the icy rush, but everything seemed to be the same as before when they gazed upwards. Their lofty palace was still bathed in turquoise serenity. The darker green of the bladder trees still brushed through their coral windows, feathering to and fro.

Then the sea-weeds were blown sideways and flattened by a sudden squall blasting the ice into the cave again, rattling the shells and the sand on the bottom in clouds . . . Then on the back of the wind they heard the faint sound of Voices, far away.

She sat up first, her dark hair tumbling over her pink-tipped human breasts. He sat up more slowly, knowing that there could be no more peace until the Call was answered. It had happened before and it would happen again, over and over, in the future.

Now they were sitting back to back on the bed with their tails waving in the water,

1

donning their white fur coats. All the while iridescent bubbles of lilac and blue and lemon floated upwards, for they were also preparing themselves to set off out of one world and into another where they would breathe the air.

The wind grew stronger, and on its wings the Voices were quite audible when they glided off towards the ominous grey North Sea. Excited and invigorated, the two beautiful creatures emerged from the depths of their cave to revel in the arctic conditions of the melting ice-fields. This was what they loved, and they paused in their frolics only when they heard the groaning from the very heart of the ocean as it began to heave and spiral and rotate.

The roaring came nearer and nearer and exploded to the top, spewing out huge racing billows that caught them and drove them on and on until they found themselves in a narrow neck of the sea, the Sound between Lerwick and the island of Bressay.

Their two white heads bobbed up out of the water to gaze at it and the town of Lerwick beyond, and they saw that the whole sea was ablaze, a vast mirror for the Northern Lights, for the fantastic colours of their myriad swaying skirts flickering across the sky.

And whenever the Merry Dancers came out to play they came with the warning that something . . . *something* was going to happen.

What?

They had no time to wonder when a gigantic roller snatched them and whirled them on through the Sound on its way to crash against the cliffs. It rose up in a monstrous green arc tipped with angry white spume, but the two seals somersaulted backwards in graceful arcs of their own, flipping their tails contemptuously as they raced off.

The Call was becoming louder and more insistent every minute.

They went on their way to answer it.

CHAPTER ONE

Three nights ago the people of Shetland could only admire the awesome display. Vibrant, electric colours exploded as the Merry Dancers swished their skirts and crackled across the heavens. But the admiration was grudging, for everyone knew such a display to be the forerunner of trouble—bad weather, perhaps, or bad news, or even Death itself.

In this case it was one almighty storm.

Looking out over the harbour of Lerwick from the window-seat of 97 Commercial Street with her sister Alice, Barbara Pitcairn saw the huge swell, screaming as it came, dash against the headland of the Knab. With her own eyes she saw what appeared to be two white seal-like creatures thrown head over heels backwards into the depths, but she had no idea that she had almost witnessed the ghosts of her life yet to come. Only fourteen years old, she could not conceive of such a thing.

It was the twenty-second day of September when the gales reached hurricane force, howling around Shetland like a thousand demented witches. They raised the sea in mountainous waves to pound the isles, to crash against the cliffs in livid arcs of green topped with white spume, and in a final gesture of evil spite to throw the spume high into the air before it rattled far inland as hard and fierce as ice crackling along the ground.

Barbara and Alice had been watching the sea in this majestic and murderous mood for two whole days now. All her life Barbara had loved to watch the boisterous waves, the sparkling plumes of spray, and listen to the noise and the fun of it all.

But today the wind had eased considerably and what fun and sparkle there had been was gone. Everything just looked cold and dreary. The sea was running off, but the black waves still pointed their fingers at her. They seemed to reach out towards her, evil and terrifying, and in spite of the warmth of the peat fire burning behind them she pulled her shawl more tightly around her shoulders and shuddered.

Now and then she was afflicted by strange feelings, always heralding the bad things in life—rarely the good—but she had never told anyone about these premonitions, not even Alice. Females with such powers were regarded as witches. Only a few years ago a witch had had the blood drawn from her 'above the breath' when the top of her head had been cut off . . . Of course she had died.

Barbara knew just by looking in the mirror that she was no witch. Her face was reassuringly pink and heart-shaped under her brown curls. She had always gone to the Kirk on Sundays, prayed for guidance every other

6

day of the week, and worked as hard as she could all the time. She had always been a good girl, but she hated the sea now, so black and angry and cruel, and she knew that she would curse it every day until their father came home.

'Have you spoken to the Aunts?' she asked Alice. 'Did you find out why Mother has taken to her bed again?'

'Oh, Barbara! You know why! It's because we haven't heard from Father for such a long time.'

'But quite often we don't hear from him, if he's on a long trip.'

'This one has been much longer than usual,' Alice said sadly, hearing the pleading in her young sister's voice. 'He should have been back long ago.'

'He's coming soon! I know he is! Perhaps today. Yes, he'll come today.' Barbara's tearful, jerky utterances betrayed her fear and anxiety. 'Anyway, I'm going to sit here all afternoon and wait for him. I'll be the first one to see his ship come in.'

Alice sighed and went to speak to Aunt Mary and Aunt Ellice again. Perhaps by now Mother would be feeling better and they would be in a more cheerful frame of mind. But she found them as gloomy as before. They shook their heads at her, which meant that nothing had changed since she had spoken to them an hour ago, and for once their hands were idle.

Aunt Mary Bruce was wearing a pretty brown silk dress and Aunt Ellice Bruce was in blue. Over their gowns were small white-flowered aprons trimmed with lace, and there was more fine lace in their caps and ruffles. Every afternoon they dressed as elegantly as this, as befitted gentle women in the fashion of 1744, hoping to receive George Pitcairn, their brother-in-law, back from the sea at last.

They were both seated on straight-backed embroidered chairs. On footstools embroidered to match, the toes of their slippers peeped out from under the hems of their gowns. They were accomplished needlewomen, and when they weren't sewing they were knitting or spinning their wool.

Aunt Mary was the expert at the spinning wheel, never satisfied until the wool was as fine and as delicate as a cobweb. Then Aunt Ellice's fingers would fly as she knitted lacy shawls out of these cobwebs, so fine that they could pass through a wedding ring. They were much sought after when now and then they became available in George Pitcairn's shop. But today the spinning wheel was still, and the wool and the knitting needles lay neglected in the straw kishie at Aunt Ellice's side.

Alice was away so long that Barbara wondered uneasily what was wrong now. In fact, she felt drawn as though by a string to the sitting room, but all she saw when she got

8

there were her sister and their two aunts, all strangely silent.

'What is it?' she cried. 'What's wrong? Is Mother all right?'

'Of course she is,' Aunt Mary said, and got to her feet. 'She's just tired, that's all. Tired of waiting. Come with me, Barbara, and see for yourself.'

It was not unusual for Mistress Babsie Pitcairn to take to her bed. She was delicate, and because her husband was away at sea so much her two sisters had come to stay, to nurse her and look after the girls. She was also the prettiest of the three Bruce sisters with her soft brown waving hair and her dimpled smile, and eighteen years ago George Pitcairn would have no one else for his wife. They were as happy as they were well-matched, and in time their first child Alice had been born, and later, Barbara. Being the captain and owner of his own brig, Mr Pitcairn was well able to look after his family of ladies. They wanted for nothing except his company.

Babsie was lying in her bed, with her eyes closed. She was so thin now with worry that her body scarcely raised the bedclothes, and her face was like white marble. Was she dead? Was that what had happened? Barbara gave a great jump and a cry when she saw her mother. Aunt Mary held her back and Babsie's eyes opened, filled with a question.

But Aunt Mary shook her head and then

bustled round the bed, hauling Babsie up on to her pillows and smoothing the sheets. 'Time to sit up, lass. Barbara will sit with you while I fetch you some broth.'

Later that day Barbara went back to the little window and watched the boats that were venturing out to sea again. When darkness came down and the oil lamps were lit she was still sitting there, straining her eyes to see the white forward light, the green starboard light and the red port light of her father's two-masted sailing ship. She could tell it a mile off, because that red light, the one she wanted to see most in all the world, always dipped a little on the left side of the brig.

Just as she stood up very reluctantly to go and join the others a ship did come into Lerwick harbour. It was single-masted, rigged fore and aft with a running bowsprit, and it was coming in fast. She had never seen it before, but she thought it might be a cutter, and she watched it docking at the pier. A company of men dressed in dark clothes disembarked swiftly. They spoke to the other men at the harbour before they formed themselves into a column to march along the street.

Their feet, marching slowly and heavily in unison, had a frightening, dolorous sound. Barbara didn't like the look of the men at all as they came nearer and nearer. They were officials of some sort, and nobody could

10

mistake that they were on bad business, very bad business indeed.

There were always foreign sailors in Lerwick. Perhaps one of them was an escaped prisoner from Norway or Denmark or some other country, she thought, and these men had come to recapture him. But as she stared at them, her heart froze in utter horror when they stopped at the house that belonged to her father, at 97 Commercial Street—*this very house*—and knocked at the door.

· Barbara flew to her sister's side. The two aunts jumped up. Aunt Mary opened the door and listened to what the men had to say. Then she began to scream and wail.

'Oh, my God! my God! Bairns, bairns, what will become of us all now? Your father's ship has gone down! George Pitcairn and all his crew are lost . . .'

*   *   *

Within the space of a few months further disaster befell the family. Although for years they had all lived with the dread that George Pitcairn might be shipwrecked or even drowned some awful day in the never-never, in the shock of its actually happening Mistress Babsie Pitcairn became incapable of eating, drinking or even speaking, and her eyes looked dead and dark long before she passed away in March, 1745.

11

Because her sisters and her daughters had expended all their time and energies in caring for her, George Pitcairn's shop in Commercial Street had also failed. It just seemed to have happened somehow when their backs were turned. But it was the very last straw. There was no longer any money coming into the house from anywhere.

The wispy cobweb shawls and the silk embroideries became things of the past. Now Aunt Mary was spinning thick yarn, and when she'd done that, she and Aunt Ellice asked Alice and Barbara to help them knit heavy socks to sell to the Dutch and German fishermen and sailors. But once the agent had taken the lion's share of the profits there was very little left for the Pitcairn ladies. They had barely enough to live on, with nothing left over for such luxuries as new clothes.

*   *   *

The winter set in suddenly and harshly in October and continued unrelenting with scarcely a period of remission until April the following year. The few bags of peat they could afford for the fires were rapidly dwindling, and the house was cold. It was so cold that neither Alice nor Barbara could get to sleep that night, and besides, they were miserably hungry. They couldn't help overhearing the conversation the two aunts were holding. Through the thin partition wall between the two bedrooms Aunt Ellice's voice was as clear as a bell.

'How much have we got left, then?'

'Almost nothing. Tomorrow morning I'll have to go down to the boats and see if any of the fishermen are kind enough to give me a fry of fish.'

'Oh, Mary! That's just plain begging!'

'Well, it's what we've come down to now. I'll take plenty of paper to hide the fish in my basket—if I get any—and if I'm early enough and no one else is in the shop I might get some fat from the butcher to bake our *brünnies*, and perhaps even a little pat of butter to spread on them. He knows the state we're in. It's hand to mouth now, Ellice.'

'Thank God Maggie Scollay comes by with a pail of milk now and then, and Davy Scollay with beremeal and a few tatties.'

'And we wouldn't even have that, don't forget, if Davy Scollay hadn't sailed with George Pitcairn when he was younger! Now you'll remember that the fire has not to be lit until ten o'clock tomorrow morning, Ellice? Then, God willing, we can fry the fish and bake the *brünnies*. But after that we'll have to let the fire die out. We can't spare the peats.'

'How long can we survive like this, Mary?'

'God alone knows.'

Aunt Ellice dissolved into tears. 'We're letting the girls down, our dearest Babsie's

13

girls.'

'The fact is, we should have been helped long ago,' Aunt Mary's firm voice assured her sister. 'Thomas Gifford of Busta is supposed to be the philanthropist and benefactor of Shetland, is he not? So why hasn't he come forward? He's related to us, besides!'

'Distantly.' Aunt Ellice modified that statement, sniffing and still crying.

'And,' Aunt Mary charged on indignantly, her voice booming, 'since he's so carried away by the high estate of Mistress Gifford, that wife of his whom he insists on calling—'

'Ah yes,' Aunt Ellice agreed with a shudder. 'Lady Elizabeth.'

'Has he forgotten altogether that George Pitcairn was a brother of Pitcairn of Muness, no less, and we ourselves are descended from that famous knight of the realm, Laurence Bruce of Cultmalendie?'

'Infamous,' Aunt Ellice corrected her with a sigh.

'The fact remains, Ellice, that our nieces are as high-born as any of the Giffords—if not more so—and Thomas Gifford should be remembering that blood is thicker than water in times of distress like this!'

As their voices droned on Alice fell asleep. But Barbara remained wide awake, waiting for some other interesting crumb of information.

'The girls are old enough to be put into service,' Aunt Mary concluded sadly. 'I can see

14

no other future for them.'

'What a terrible downcome for us all! But what other way could they earn a living? And another question—where? Oh, Mary, I hope they will not have to be separated! They have been together all their lives.'

For a long time after their gentle snoring was all that could be heard through the partition, Barbara lay awake thinking about Thomas Gifford, the Laird of Busta. The important word there, of course, was 'Laird', a man who owned great tracts of land and the tenants on it. There were good lairds and bad lairds, but up to now she had always been under the impression that he was good and kind, even if he was a landlord.

As soon as she heard movements in the next bedroom the following morning, Barbara got up and dressed in a flash. It was still quite dark and the house was colder than ever. She wrapped herself in a shawl on top of her clothes and tied it in a knot behind her waist.

'It's not even six o'clock yet,' Aunt Ellice told her when she appeared in the kitchen.

'I know. I thought I would go down along the boats for you this morning, Aunt Mary.'

'You! A peerie thing o' a lass like you—go down along the boats!' Her scandalised aunt almost choked. 'Certainly not!'

'She means you would be in danger. You're too young and innocent to know how to deal with rough sailors and fishermen,' Aunt Ellice

15

explained.

'My own father was a sailor, and he wasn't rough,' Barbara said with tears in her eyes. 'I was only trying to help. At least let me carry your basket, Aunt Mary.'

'Well . . .' her aunt said. 'I suppose there can be no harm in that, so long as I am with you. Go and put on your outside shawl, then.'

Barbara ran to get her heavy shawl, pulling it up over her cap, and while she was knotting it at the front this time she overheard the whispers of her aunts.

'Everyone knows she is one of the orphaned Pitcairn bairns,' Aunt Mary was saying, 'so there may be a better chance of getting some fish. The men will be sorry for her.'

'You'll get the fish, no doubt of that!' Aunt Ellice sighed. 'She may be only small and slim, but she is also very pretty, and that's what counts, with men.'

Never before had Barbara been reminded so forcibly of her own femininity, one girl against a whole world of predatory men. She should be frightened. But she wasn't. It was a grown-up game, an exciting game, and the prospect of it made the blood pound in her veins like the waves of the sea.

She could hardly wait to play it.

CHAPTER TWO

In the early morning the moon was still in the sky when Thomas Gifford set off from his mansion house of Busta to go to Lerwick. His mare cantered along the tracks at an easy pace and he patted her head from time to time as he rode. She was a fine chestnut, the best horse he had ever had, which was why he had named her after his dearest wife, Betty, as he called her in private.

He watched the moon becoming a paper moon and then transparent before it disappeared altogether in the darkest hour, the hour before the dawn. Travelling southeast they passed through the village of Voe, making good time, and then came the worst part of the journey. A few grey fingers of light streaked across the heavens as they entered the long straight path through the dreaded Kames, with the shadowy hills and moors on his left side and the ghastly water-logged peatbogs on his right.

They stank to high heaven, and not for the first time Thomas Gifford thought they were a miasma of pure evil. In the growing light ghostly grey mists swirled up out of the bogs, encircling him and his horse and, as always happened there, Betty's ears were pricked in terror and alarm.

Thomas Gifford's sweaty palms held on to the reins tightly while he murmured endearments and encouragement to the mare. 'Now, my Betty! My Betty! My Betty! I'm here with you, lass. Nothing will happen to you while I am here!'

But it took him all his time and all his courage. Whenever he entered this haunted place he always became depressed. There was always the reminder here of mortality, and it was inevitable that every time he passed through it he dwelt on the five dearest and most beloved children in the world whom he and his wife had lost almost six years ago.

First, poor little Bess and Frankie had taken to bed with the smallpox. Then Thomas, James and Barbara. Their little gravestones, lovingly tended, were at the family burial ground at the Olnafirth Kirk, and as he brooded on them the tears simply poured out of his eyes, tears he tried his best never to allow his wife to witness, for it would only upset her all over again . . .

Then, thank God, they were out of the Kames at last. Betty whisked her tail and sped alongside the Loch of Girlsta and soon they were passing through Gott, up hill and down dale, round the narrow hairpin bend at the Brig o' Fitch, on and on until, as dawn broke, they came to the North Road leading into Lerwick.

There he reined in the mare and sat gazing

18

at the massed masts of the fleet in the harbour, a heartening sight in his determination to promote the fishing trade. Indeed, that was his business here today, along with all the other things claiming his attention.

Betty trotted sedately down the North Road and into Commercial Street, and Thomas Gifford was bowing to left and right at any of the people up early enough to be going about their errands, when he found himself looking down at Miss Mary Bruce of Mr Pitcairn's house. Not for a minute could he ever have suspected that his appearance was to her like that of the angel Gabriel, for she was standing stock-still in his path regarding him with her lips tight and her face cold.

'So it's you, is it, Mr Gifford?' she ground out, scarcely inclining her head.

Sensing something very untoward he slithered down from the mare to speak to her, although he could tell it was not going to be a happy encounter. There was a young girl standing beside her holding a basket. He wondered if she were one of George Pitcairn's daughters, and came to the conclusion that she must be, because she was so like Babsie, her mother. And Babsie had been a beauty in her day, the belle of Lerwick. This girl had the same fresh colouring, the same shining hair, but instead of the blue eyes of her mother, hers were golden-brown, dancing and faintly roguish. Flirtatious, in fact.

'Good morning, Miss Mary. And this must be—'

'Barbara Pitcairn, sir. A relative of your own.'

'Yes . . . A terrible tragedy, Miss Barbara. You have my deepest sympathy.' Searching for something appropriate to add to this, he went on. 'And how old are you, my dear?'

'She will be sixteen on Midsummer's Day, sir,' Aunt Mary said before Barbara could open her mouth. 'Her older sister, Alice, is already sixteen, coming to seventeen.'

It was at this point that Thomas Gifford saw the tell-tale fish under the paper covering the basket and deduced at once that these two had been at the boats begging.

Aunt Mary followed his gaze and flushed angrily. 'Yes, sir! We have come down to this! George Pitcairn's income dried up long ago. No longer is 97 Commercial Street a warm, comfortable house and, as you can see, even our gowns have become very dilapidated.' She held up her ragged hem which Barbara thought was a bit unfair, for Aunt Mary had donned her very oldest working dress that morning, no doubt on purpose.

'But there is still George Pitcairn's shop, surely?' he gasped.

'Failed,' Aunt Mary said, pretending to sway dramatically as she grasped Barbara's arm to steady herself. 'But now you must excuse us, sir, for your own sake. It would not do if the

20

residents of Lerwick saw the Laird of Busta merely passing the time of day with his impoverished relatives. Tongues would wag, as you know, and we would not wish to bring your great name into disrepute, considering all your other acts of generosity towards the Shetland people.' Hurrying Barbara away she added, 'Good day, sir.'

With that she swept on and Thomas Gifford began his long day of business, sadly interrupted in the afternoon by his brother, Andrew Gifford of Ollaberry. As usual, he had come to beg for money, and this irritated Thomas even more than usual on a day when he was already consumed with worry.

'Our parents gave all their children the same chance,' he berated his brother. 'Because you choose to drink day and night, and fornicate all over the countryside, you only have yourself to blame.'

'Believe me, you are the last man I would ever approach,' Andrew said, with a spark of hatred in his voice. Then he changed his tune to a whine. 'But nobody else I've asked has one drop of Christian charity in his veins.'

'I'm not surprised,' Thomas snapped.

Andrew became desperate. 'Brother,' he begged, 'I'm depending on you! At least send us some mutton so that the bairns do not starve!'

This appeal on behalf of the children never failed to persuade Thomas Gifford, as Andrew

21

of Ollaberry very well knew. 'It will be the last,' Thomas swore, and threw him out.

He didn't see that, once outside the council chambers, Ollaberry straightened up and even swaggered as he jingled the last few coins in his pocket, intending to buy a few drinks to give him Dutch courage to visit that plump little widow who lived in a but on the North Road.

But as Thomas Gifford galloped back wearily to Busta that evening he caught sight of his brother's horse half-hidden behind the hut that was gaining quite a reputation. His thoughts were very uneasy, and became more and more so on his way back through the Kames.

How could his beloved Andrina, his favourite daughter, become so infatuated with a second-generation rogue like Patrick Gifford, her cousin? For what else could the boy be, with that wastrel, Andrew, for a father? Quite apart from the terrible problem of consanguinity? He had lectured Andrina about the probability of all her children being mentally retarded as the result of marrying her first cousin, but it had made no difference.

When he shed tears this time returning through the Kames they were tears of frustration. To do his best for his family was his first priority, but he objected strongly to keeping two families, as his ne'er-do-well of a brother would have him do. At this rate, no

22

matter how hard he worked, he would have very little to leave to his own children.

To do his very best for the Shetlanders, especially his tenants, was his second priority. Everyone knew that, he thought angrily as he galloped home, but now, after those few well-aimed darts from Miss Mary Bruce this morning, he realised that his unsullied reputation could well be in grave danger.

To tell the truth, he had been uneasy from the minute he had heard of George Pitcairn's disaster. Now that he had learned that his shop had gone as well as his ship, he was extremely alarmed. Of course, there could be no money, no firing, no wool to knit and very little food to eat for the Pitcairn ladies. Something would have to be done for the two orphaned girls, his own distant relatives. It should have been seen to long ago. They were only young girls, especially that delightful Barbara. But what? Well . . . they were of an age to work, he mused, and then he had his brilliant idea. They could work at Busta. But there was the rub, indeed . . . How could he persuade his wife to take two outsiders into their own private nest? Even if, by Shetland standards, it was almost a castle?

*   *   *

A week later he put his foot down, to end his wife's sniffs and snarls and arguments. It

23

wasn't often that his chin went up in such an aggressive manner, or his blue eyes flashed so icily, or his fist banged down with such a thump on the table. She recognised danger at once and snapped her mouth shut in a long, tight line.

'I must not be found wanting where my own relations are concerned,' he boomed, 'considering my reputation for generosity towards those worse off than ourselves. Not to mention your reputation either, my dear, you who are known as Lady Bountiful.'

His wife turned her head away to hide a smirk, nodding haughtily in agreement. She saw it as very much to her advantage to distribute largesse, but she never saw that the gentle, independent people hated such charity, almost as much as they despised her for lording it over them.

'Besides,' Mr Gifford went on, 'the two girls may help to fill the gaps in our own family in some very small way.'

It was as though he had pierced her with a dagger. He could not have presented his case in a worse manner. 'You cannot mean to adopt them as our own children?' she gasped. 'After providing you with fourteen beautiful children you have cut me to the heart, Thomas Gifford. It was not my fault that our five little souls passed away,' and she sobbed bitterly, well aware that her tears were her most powerful tool.

Thomas Gifford softened immediately. 'Of course not, my dearest Betty. You have been—you are—the best mother any children could ever possibly have. As for the Pitcairn lasses, they are only poor relations and distant ones at that, to be kept in their place. But it is my duty to give them food and shelter. The Shetland people will certainly think so.'

'Let them be maidservants, then,' she ground out.

Maidservants! Ignoring his wife's sullen expression Thomas Gifford pretended to be delighted with this idea, resolving that he would integrate the Pitcairn girls into the family later, once his wife had got used to them. 'Now that you have solved the problem for me, my darling, as you solve so many, I will arrange transport for them to be taken here as soon as possible. The first day of June, would you say?'

'If you must,' she conceded with a face like a dish of sour milk. 'But you will not use the coach for such a purpose. They can have the use of the horse and cart. That's how servants travel. Or on foot.'

She knew when she was beaten. For the present. She didn't want those girls here. She wouldn't make it easy for them when they got here, and then they might go back to Lerwick where they belonged.

*   *   *

Besides being the most forward-thinking, competent and intelligent man of his day in Shetland, Thomas Gifford was also meticulous, an extremely well-organised perfectionist. In the same way that he thought through matters of state, commerce, the instigation of education for the children of the Isles and business ventures down to the very last detail, he turned his attention now to this small domestic matter which had been brought to his attention—and held there, he had to admit, by two dancing brown eyes.

He sat at his desk and studied his map of Shetland, which he knew off by heart already. But he never took anything for granted. These Pitcairn girls could not be expected to ride— even if they could ride, which he doubted—all the way to Busta House. In a cart, as his wife insisted, it would be a bumpy, arduous journey on the almost non-existent roads. No! In a spell of settled weather, the greatest part of their journey should be made by sea. That was the easiest way.

And yes, he was right! The shortest way from Lerwick on the east coast of the Shetland Mainland to Busta to the north-west side, would be to travel to the most north-westerly setting-off point, at Aith. From there to Busta there were plenty of small isles and inlets on the way to rest or run for shelter should, by any chance, the weather deteriorate.

                    *   *   *

Within another week a cart arrived at 97 Commercial Street from Busta and was unloaded, the most perishable and delicate goods first. There was a hen dressed ready to roast, a side of lamb and twelve bags of peats to cook them with, raw wool to be spun and potatoes and vegetables, luxuries the Pitcairn ladies had almost forgotten.

'Oh, my God!' Aunt Mary exclaimed. 'A hen! And mutton we can smoke in the peat-reek! We have food here to last us for many a long day!'

'And here is a message from Mr Gifford,' the carter said before he went away to deliver another load, this time to Ollaberry.

'Oh, Alice . . . Barbara! Oh, my dears!' Aunt Ellice sobbed with shock and gratitude. 'Mr Gifford has sent for you. He has arranged that Peter Williamson, one of the best sailors in Shetland, will take you by boat from Aith. You are to go and live at Busta House! Just imagine—'

'When?' Barbara asked, trying not to sound eager. But she knew that a great adventure was about to begin.

'I don't want to go,' moaned Alice.

'You will set off at eight o'clock on the morning of the first of June,' Aunt Mary told them, ignoring Alice and consulting the

27

calendar. 'That's in only six weeks, six weeks on Saturday. With this wool we can knit you new shawls and new fine spencer-vests to wear under your gowns when it is cold. The dresses themselves will be the problem, for you have both entirely grown out of the ones you possess.'

'There are still the trunks of materials their father used to bring home for Babsie,' Aunt Ellice ventured.

'Of course!' A relieved Aunt Mary agreed, and then assumed command as usual. 'Well, there is plenty to do, more than enough within the space of six weeks. Ellice, show them the materials. They must have two new night-gowns and two new day-gowns each—more if we can manage them, and in the meantime I shall start spinning the wool.'

*   *   *

On the last evening of May, by dint of sheer hard work and determination, Aunt Mary and Aunt Ellice had the two girls ready to leave. Everything had to be spotless. Even now the last gossamer shawl was pegged out by its points to the large square wooden shawl-stretcher propped up against the wall beside the fire, and the two aunts had been underlining decorum for hours, very boring hours for Barbara, who was impatient to start their new life, and for Alice who grew more apprehensive by the minute.

Finally, before they all went to bed that last night, Aunt Mary said sternly, 'Now, there are politics, a subject which your father quite rightly considered should not concern us ladies. But remember, you are about to enter the home and the very heart of Shetland politics, and your Aunt Ellice and I consider you should not do so unadvised.'

'Yes, Aunt,' Barbara and Alice droned.

'Absolute power is given to the lords of the realm from the monarch. In Shetland's case the Earl of Morton holds the Lordship Estate, which gives him the title of Earl of Zetland as well.

'He has made Thomas Gifford his stand-in, to be the Sheriff, the Chamberlain and the Admiral here. Naturally, Mr Gifford is a King's man, a Whig and a supporter of the Hanoverian succession.'

'All the other lairds are Jacobites and Tories,' Aunt Ellice put in nervously, 'but if you take our advice you will pretend not to understand any of it. Just don't discuss it, and above all, don't let Mistress Gifford intimidate you. You are as good as she is if not better.'

When the girls managed to go to bed at last, tears poured down Alice's pale face. 'I don't want to go,' she sobbed. 'I'm frightened of the sea voyage, and I'm frightened of Busta House and everyone in it, especially that old Mistress Gifford.'

Barbara hugged her sister until she calmed down and finally fell asleep. Soon, the two aunts were sleeping, too, tired out by all their hard work, but Barbara's eyes were sparkling so much at the prospect of such an adventure that she thought they would never close that night.

*   *   *

Thomas Gifford's arrangements went like clockwork. At ten o'clock on Saturday morning the horse and cart drew up at 97 Commercial Street, and Alice clung to her aunts, bidding them a tearful farewell. Barbara handed their boxes and bags over to the driver and then kissed her aunts goodbye, almost in tears herself.

'One last word,' Aunt Mary said, fiercely embracing each one in turn, 'if you don't like living at Busta you must come back home at once. Your Aunt Ellice and I will stay on here and keep the place for you. It is still, and always will be, your home.'

Barbara wondered what on earth made Aunt Mary say a thing like that when she and Alice were on their way to a beautiful home and a better future. Surely the aunts knew they would never come back!

Alice cheered up a little on their slow, trundling journey in the cart. Neither of them had been outside Lerwick before, and they marvelled at the hills and lochs and the sea which was always around the next corner.

'Ay,' the driver smiled at them, 'in Shetland you're never more than two miles from the sea wherever you go.' It was true. The sea invaded the land in long, shining fingers, and the short green grass was studded pink with thrift. 'They call those long inlets voes,' the driver added. 'They are miniature versions of the fjords in Norway, only there they are deeper and wider and covered with trees right down to the water. Many a time I've sailed up and down them, in my younger day.'

Almost before they knew it they were in Aith, where Peter Williamson and his son, Samuel, were waiting in their boat for them at the pier.

'You're right on time,' Mr Williamson said, as he and Samuel stowed away the luggage.

Barbara kept back the last basket and she and Alice sat down on the grass. 'Let's have a picnic,' she said, waving a hand to invite the two men to sit down beside them. 'Aunt Ellice has put three bottles of *blaand* in here, enough for us all. She was getting the whey of the buttermilk ready all day yesterday. It's at the sparkling stage, now.'

She handed out the bottles and the glasses while Alice opened a white cloth containing the beremeal cakes fresh baked that morning and spread thickly with butter. 'Have a *brünnie*,' she said shyly, 'and after that there

31

are some apple tarts.'

An hour or two later the sea voyage began on a beautiful afternoon, soft and balmy with a light southerly wind. Soon the men put up the sail and they skimmed along. Even timid Alice forgot her fears. The sun glittered on the water so that it danced with sparkles of silver, and every now and then a puffin popped up at the side of the boat with its striped parrot beak and bright inquisitive eyes, wanting them to play with him.

'Ho, ho, Tammie Norie,' Barbara called and they waited until the odd, comical little creature swam under the boat and popped up again at the other side to make Alice smile, and even laugh.

'Where are we now?' Barbara asked Mr Williamson as the afternoon wore on.

'Between Papa Little and the Mainland, heading towards Busta Voe. We should be there in another hour.'

They passed by deep dark caves and steep narrow gullies which Samuel told them were called geos, whose only visitors were the sea birds. They saw banks on top of cliffs so worn away by the sea that they had no backs to them. Any unwary person could walk on top of those dangerous crumbling edges and fall to his death. But Busta Voe was long and as smooth as glass when they glided into it at last.

'The House will be coming into sight on our left side shortly,' Mr Williamson said. 'Over there, on the right side, is Wethersta. Some distant relations of Thomas Gifford, also called Gifford, live there in that old mansion house. His sons often row across the Voe to visit the family.'

At the very mention of the word 'Wethersta' black wings seemed to flap right over Barbara's head. She was conscious that the sun was still shining, and the water was still unruffled when inexplicably a great shudder went right through her, and she was gripped by the most terrible black fear of her life. It gripped her heart. The blood drained from her head and her face. Her arms, her legs, her whole body became powerless in this dark place.

She knew it was a place of death.

She thought she was going to die, herself.

CHAPTER THREE

In two strides Mr Williamson was across the boat to Barbara's side. He took her limp, ice-cold hands in his and stared anxiously into her face. He could tell she wasn't fainting, nor was she having a fit of some kind, but she was far away in some dreadful place which only she could see.

'What is it, lass?' he asked her gently. 'Surely you're not seasick, not now at the last of it?'

Very gradually the dark, evil mists began to swirl around Barbara, swirl and then part to let in first one shaft of sunlight, and then another, and another. Some feeling came back to her skin. She felt Mr Williamson's rough hands grating against hers as he tried to rub some warmth back into them, until she came back from somewhere else to this boat, to this very moment when the sky was still azure blue, the sea was changing in the turquoise of shallower waters, and the blood of her life flooded back into her veins again.

'No, not sick,' she whispered. 'It was only a goose walking over my grave.'

'Or a white seal,' she heard Samuel say, and then shout as he peered into the water. 'Look, Father! They always said that the white seals lived here. They're everywhere!'

Mr Williamson did not pick up the oars immediately, but sat looking at her with a serious expression. 'What did you see?' he asked.

'Nothing. It was only a feeling of such a cold, sad place.'

'Perhaps you have the Second Sight,' he said. 'There is a legend about this place, did you know? Busta House is supposed to be cursed.'

He rowed on quietly, and it came into view, a great, grey brooding house with smooth walls.

'What curse?'

'Well, lass, years ago some old man was convinced of injustice at the hands of a Gifford and cursed the family from here to Hell, prophesying that no son would ever inherit Busta, and if he did, he would wish that he were dead. But of course it is impossible in the present family. Thomas and Mistress Gifford lost three sons in the smallpox outbreak, but four sons survived. Even if one of them met with an accident and died today, there would still be three others left.'

He guided the boat alongside a very fine jetty, cast up a rope and Samuel climbed the steps to secure it to a ring. 'I'll throw up some of the boxes out of your way,' his father smiled at the girls, 'so that you can reach the bottom step.'

The first thing to meet their gaze was a thickness of trees—real trees, with real trunks and real branches and real, fluttering green leaves. Life came back to Barbara in a rush.

'Look, Alice! Trees!'

They had never seen one before. They could scarcely believe their eyes. So many green leaves, stubby to be sure, and the tree trunks stunted, short and gnarled—but trees!

Thomas Gifford saw the girls with their backs towards him, and remembered that Alice was the name of the older one. Although she was much bigger than the dainty little Barbara, she appeared to droop in a disconsolate manner. Perhaps she was shy, he thought.

'You are admiring the glade, I see.' The girls whirled around to see Mr Gifford and a much taller young man beside him. 'You are welcome here, both of you. Let me introduce you to my oldest son, John.' The girls curtsied. John Gifford nodded his head briefly. 'Just leave your luggage!' Mr Gifford commanded next. 'It will be seen to. Before we move off I should point out those small twin buildings on your left. One is the dovecote and the other the summer-house. We are all very fond of them. In fine weather the summer-house is a pleasant place to sit and listen to the doves whirring in and out.'

'But aren't they very near the edge of the cliffs?' Alice cast them a terrified glance, while Barbara waved farewell to Samuel and his father Peter Williamson who had been so kind to her.

'Nonsense!' Mr Gifford squashed Alice with a word, and she hung her head. 'Now then, since you are attracted by the trees, we will approach the house by that way,' and he struck out along a path that led through them. 'We call this the Willow Walk,' he said, walking and talking rapidly as he explained why his ancestor had ever planted the glade of trees in the first place so far north of the tree belt, and how the high enclosing walls had protected them from the Shetland weather. It was only the tops of them, as they could see, which were blasted sideways by the wind.

While he was speaking Alice trailed along beside them with her head still bent. Barbara hoped she wasn't crying again, while she herself studied the great Laird of Busta at close quarters—which wasn't easy at the rate he was going.

He was short and rotund, but very brisk, with penetrating blue eyes, and now that he wasn't wearing a wig, she saw that what hair he had left on his head was turning grey. Under his dark blue coat he wore a ruffled white shirt and a snow-white cravat, and he was spotlessly turned out to the points of his black leather shoes. He was not imposing, but there was an air about him which commanded respect and Barbara concluded in this brief appraisal that even if she had not been warned, she would still have known at once that here was a very clever man. Furthermore, he did not stand still in one place for long, and was used to giving out orders and having them promptly obeyed.

She was even more interested in his son who never uttered a word while he walked along languidly at their other side, dressed impeccably in high fashion, in grey. He wore a silk hat on top of his dark hair and carried a silver-topped cane. He was every inch a gentleman, and Barbara was very impressed. It was the first time she had ever seen such a dandy.

Many times she had gazed out of their window in Lerwick at the large, blond young Norwegian sailors in their heavy fishermen's ganzies and her heart had skipped a beat, but never before had she seen as handsome a man as John Gifford. Never before had she seen smudgy grey eyes like his, smouldering, beautiful eyes. But to judge from his stern, silent profile she thought that he must be very unhappy . . .

She felt quite breathless when they reached the cultivated grasslands surrounding the House of Busta and looked up at its walls. They were built of grey boulders cemented together with smooth mortar, high and infinitely forbidding. She especially disliked the uneven windows, one here, one there, in no sort of order, and assumed that they were all so small and so mean in order to avoid the glass tax. They resembled crooked little eyes, which more than anything else lent the house an air of mystery, of suspicion, and of secrets locked deep inside. Feeling totally repelled, Barbara was once again overcome by the same dread that had visited her in the Voe.

'Many ladies are not good sailors even on flat calm seas,' Mr Gifford was saying. He must have noticed her pallor, for he was holding her arm. 'They feel the land swaying long after they disembark. You will be perfectly restored in the morning after a good night's sleep. Perhaps you would like to go straight upstairs?'

'If you please, Mr Gifford,' Alice said faintly.

'But before we go inside I must show you something,' he said, grasping John's cane and pointing above the door with it. 'These are the combined coats of arms of the Giffords of Busta and those of my wife who was the daughter of Sir Andrew Mitchell of Westshore,' he said proudly.

It was a square stone set into the walls of the house. Once it had been elaborately carved, but now it was green-mossed and crumbling after years of withstanding salt-laden gales. Barbara could not decide what the creature's head was which dominated it. It might have been a stag, or a horned ram, but with its head turned to the side like that, it looked as though it had the huge, cruel beak of an eagle.

'My wife's emblem,' Mr Gifford said, tapping it, and Barbara smiled politely, repressing another shudder as they entered a door protected by a small porch. She was more interested in how their boxes came to be waiting for them inside. Somebody must have carried them up here by a different route. Somehow she wasn't surprised. Mr Gifford would have organised all that. He could organise anything, she now believed.

He seemed struck by a second thought. 'It was a flat calm, was it, all the way? It has been a beautiful day here, but the weather and the sea can both be so capricious, even from district to district in these isles.'

'It was very . . . interesting,' Barbara replied.

The house was quiet and still, and nobody else came to meet them. 'I'll go and fetch a maidservant. They are all sure to be in the kitchen at this time of night getting the evening meal ready,' Mr Gifford said. 'She will show you where to go,' and he bustled off through a door out of which the smell of food greasily cooking wafted out. It was mutton, Barbara thought, Alice's pet hate.

'We will dine in an hour,' Mr Gifford said when he returned a minute later with a young country girl who smiled shyly. 'Now then, Kitty,' he beetled down his brows at the servant, 'these are the Misses Pitcairn who have come to stay with us. No doubt, in time, they will fit in to the routine of the household and be happy to take up duties of their own. They are relatives of mine and so you are to address them as Miss Alice and Miss Barbara.'

'Yes sir,' Kitty said, dipping in a curtsy.

'Well, well—start taking up their luggage, then!'

'Yes, sir.'

Barbara spoke up. 'We should be happy if you and Mistress Gifford would excuse us this evening, sir, although of course we will join you in the morning. The journey has tired us out.'

'Yes, Father,' John spoke for the first time. 'They have had a long, tiring day in the heat of the sun. Perhaps something light should be sent up to them before they go to bed?' His voice was very deep and very masculine, and it sent a little thrill through Barbara to think that a real gentleman had thought of their well-being.

'Perfectly understandable,' Mr Gifford nodded his head. 'But one thing, my dears, before you go—'

'Yes, sir?' Barbara and Alice replied together.

'Although my wife is always referred to formally as Lady Busta, you may address her as Lady Elizabeth, since you are here on her special invitation. Of course, for most purposes, you will simply say, "Yes, my lady" or "No, my lady", and she will appreciate your curtsies to her.'

His eyes remained as blue and as steady and as kindly as ever, and Barbara and Alice dropped stunned little curtsies to him. They were completely astounded. They had been born and bred in the land of gentle manners, where courtesy was automatic. They had never been faced with pomp and ceremony of any kind in Shetland before.

'Of course, sir,' they said gravely.

But as they climbed the staircase curving between austerely whitewashed walls behind Kitty, who had come back down to show them

41

the way and collect the rest of the baggage, Barbara felt chilled and unwelcome. Nobody in her own family would have dreamed of serving a meal of greasy mutton to any ladies fresh off a sea voyage. They would have shown much more respect, not only for the ladies, but also for their stomachs. Little warning bells were sounding in her head already. All the respect in this house must be directed towards the most important person in it, and that was undoubtedly the eagle-woman, Mistress Gifford.

Or rather, Lady Elizabeth.

*   *   *

Carrying a bag or a box in each hand the three girls climbed up and up. Up and up they toiled until, puffing and panting, they arrived at the top of the house, in the attics.

Kitty smiled at them. 'We're so glad you've come! When do you start? Tomorrow morning? No, that's Sunday . . . Monday, perhaps? Well, don't worry—I'll keep you right.'

'Alice and I were sent for, that's all we know. We don't know what will be expected of us.'

'Well, you've been put into the attics, haven't you? That means the mistress expects you to be her servants, the same as us.'

'Then you sleep up here, too?' Barbara asked.

'Oh, no. All the maids live round about and go home after the evening meal. But you'll see us again in the morning.'

'Both attics have been got ready,' Barbara said, going from one to the other, seeing how tiny they were with room only for a narrow bed and a cupboard.

'Yes, Miss Barbara. I got them ready for you, and I fetched two little mirrors from home to put on each windowsill. You don't have dressing-tables, I'm afraid.' The windowsills were deep, the mirrors were tiny, but beside each mirror Kitty had placed a small glass with the pink flowers of thrift in it. She had done her best. 'I suppose you'll be seeing Lady Elizabeth tomorrow, as well,' she added, as if in warning.

Alice burst into tears. Kitty rushed to put her arms around her. 'Oh, I didn't mean to upset you! Don't cry, Miss Alice,' she said. 'Miss Christina will be there as well.'

'Miss Christina?' Alice asked. 'Who's she?'

'A daughter, the only Gifford girl living here now. All the others are married. Even Miss Andrina has gone away . . .'

'Miss Andrina, Kitty?' Barbara sensed that the maidservant was bursting to tell them about her.

'She wants to marry her cousin,' Kitty told them with relish. 'Oh, my! For such a scandal! Even if Patrick Gifford is too good-looking to be true! Of course her father and mother

43

forbade it, so she ran away and lives with one or other of her sisters now. Please don't tell Miss Christina I told you. Miss Christina's very nice. She's on our side.'

'On our side, Kitty?' Barbara raised her eyebrows.

'She tries to see that we are treated fairly, Miss Barbara. She doesn't always see eye to eye with her mother, either. Sometimes I think she's desperate to leave Busta, but although lots of men have asked her to marry them, she's refused every one.'

'And John Gifford?' Barbara asked. 'Is he married?'

'John Gifford is the apple of his mother's eye and the heir to this estate,' Kitty said. 'If Mr Gifford died and John were married, Lady Elizabeth would be the Dowager. She would have to get out of Busta House in favour of his bride. She wouldn't like that.'

'So she is a very proud lady?'

'But not all bad,' Kitty hastened to say. 'She wouldn't object to the other boys marrying. Their brides would be no threat to her. But she keeps John on a very right rein. She's keeping him single as long as she can.'

'Yes,' Barbara recalled. 'Mr Williamson told us there were four Gifford boys altogether.'

'Robert is the next oldest to John. Then, William. And last of all everyone's favourite, Hay. Hay's fourteen and full of mischief. Anyway, I'll go downstairs now and fetch you

44

up a cool drink and something to eat,' Kitty said, and while they were waiting for her to come back Alice and Barbara unpacked and looked around their sleeping quarters.

'I hate it here,' Alice wept.

Barbara could see that this would be another night when Alice cried herself to sleep if she didn't stay with her and try to comfort her. She shook out her Sunday dress for her and hung it up. Then she unrolled Alice's own lacy shawl which Aunt Ellice had carefully packed in black tissue paper, and later that night she saw her into her bed, held her hand, and waited until her sister fell asleep.

*   *   *

The sun had set in its glory of scarlet and gold, and dusk had been and gone in breathtaking pinks and lilacs shot through with green, and now the short Shetland night closed down on Busta Voe, darkly purple and finally inky blue. Barbara stood at the small window in her own attic and looked down the Voe, stretching shadowy and calm, and wondered which rooms the Giffords were in at that moment.

Did they look out this same way? Or did they look back into the hills, eastwards into the moon? Just then a ray lit up the waters, a long shaft of brilliance that changed everything into a fairyland of hills melting into hills beyond, and beyond that again into an eternity, and

45

everywhere she looked they were ringed by the shining sea.

And as she stood there dreaming at the window a little boat stole out from below the Willow Walk. Four oars streaked silently through the still waters, hardly causing a ripple, and something told Barbara that nobody was supposed to know about this little expedition.

She made out John sitting in the bow. She knew him by his hat. Of course, being so special, he wasn't rowing. His three brothers must have three of the oars so who had the other one? It wouldn't be Mr Gifford himself at this time of night. He would be in his bed.

So there must be another man living at Busta, one Kitty had forgotten to mention.

Who was he?

CHAPTER FOUR

Next morning Barbara dressed right up to her petticoats and bent her head down low to begin the long, tedious business of brushing her hair out, every strand. Once she had got this over with she could put on her new Sunday gown which Aunt Mary had made out of sprigged muslin with narrow damson stripes, and arrange the tiny lace cap slotted with damson ribbons on the top of her head.

And as she brushed, she could not help the little question which had been bothering her all night coming out into the light of day, on this gloriously sunny morning. Why had none of the family come to see them last night? They must all have known that she and Alice had arrived, yet here they were still marooned up in these attics, without any idea of how to get to the dining room—or any other room— in this huge, unfriendly house.

Then there was a quiet knock and a strange voice asked, 'May I come in?'

Barbara threw down her hairbrush and opened the door.

'My dear,' said the small, fair lady standing there, 'I am Christina Gifford. The maids are busy in the kitchen, so I have come to fetch you both downstairs myself. Which one are you? Alice or Barbara?'

'Barbara, Miss Christina. It's very kind of you to come for us. I'm almost ready—and here's Alice now,' she answered when her sister joined them, looking very nervous and wearing an identical gown except that the stripes were yellow.

'How are you both? Have you recovered?'

So that was it of course, Barbara thought, and felt slightly better. Nobody had wanted to disturb them last night.

'Thank you, Miss Christina. We were only a little giddy, coming off the sea,' Alice answered, a little colour coming back into her cheeks, and Barbara could tell that her sister liked Christina, right from the start. Her appearance was so very reassuring, a feminine version of her father, Thomas Gifford, with her direct blue eyes and kindly smile.

'You will have some breakfast?' she asked them. 'Do you feel well enough?'

'Oh yes, Miss Christina,' Alice said while Barbara fixed the last pin in her cap.

'Then follow me. We will probably be alone in the dining room, at least to start with. Father will have eaten long ago, and the other men will not be up yet.' After a little pause Christina added, 'They were out late last night.'

They were indeed, thought Barbara, as they seated themselves at the polished dining table. Where? And who went with them? The room was low-beamed with small, bright windows staring far out over the Voe, and now that the dreaded moment was almost upon them, Alice began to tremble. 'And Lady Elizabeth?' she asked anxiously.

'My mother has breakfast in her own room, dear. Now, what will you have? Will you start with porridge?'

They were drinking a cup of tea afterwards, and Barbara had come to the conclusion that Christina Gifford was older than she had seemed at first—in her mid-twenties even—when the door opened and a tall, dark young man came in, dressed all in black. From this, and the round white collar above his cravat, they deduced that he was a minister of the Gospel.

'No, ladies—pray remain seated,' he said, as they half rose in deference to his cloth. 'You are the Pitcairn girls, I take it?'

'This is the Reverend John Fisken,' Christina said, introducing them.

Alice inclined her head shyly and Barbara extended her hand. 'We are pleased to make your acquaintance, sir.'

'And I yours,' he said, and seated himself.

There was silence for a short time while Mr Fisken got through a large dish of porridge and then proceeded to some cold boiled fish. This he ate along with two large bannocks liberally spread with butter, and helped down with several large mugs of milk.

'You are thirsty this morning?' Christina asked.

'Last night was quite boisterous at Wethersta,' he admitted with a smile, and from that Barbara deduced that he had been the fifth man in the boat going to Wethersta, and when they had got there they had had too much to drink. His breakfast was almost finished before the ladies had sipped their small cups of tea.

'You are in a hurry today, of course,' Christina said, as if she had to say something to excuse him.

'I am indeed,' he grinned. 'Lady Elizabeth

wishes me to hear her devotions in private before I go to take the service.'

Then he was off like a whirlwind and Christina shook her head in annoyance. 'Really!' she exclaimed. 'There is nothing wrong with my mother. She is only staying in bed because she can't be bothered to get up, but as usual she has everyone running about after her, anyway. Poor John Fisken! He doesn't have much of a life here, I'm afraid. She makes him sing for his supper.'

'Sing for his supper, Miss Christina?'

'Oh, my mother makes him do a lot of things which she should do herself, really, like visiting the sick, for example, and as well as all his other duties he acts as tutor to my younger brothers.' With this remark Christina led the way back upstairs to get ready for the Kirk. They met three young men galloping down, all in various stages of undress, buttoning their shirt cuffs or donning their coats.

'This is Robert. We call him Robbie,' Christina introduced the oldest one, a little younger than herself, but fair as she was, tall and extremely handsome. He smiled pleasantly, very sleepy-eyed.

'And this is William.' William was shorter and a good deal younger, perhaps eighteen, and the image of the Laird of Busta.

'And Hay . . . Really, Hay,' Christina sighed, 'you will have to do better than that, dear. Have you combed your hair at all this morning?'

Barbara liked Hay best of all. He would be as tall and good-looking as Robert some day. But now he was only a boy, with the smile of a wicked angel.

'I'll comb it, Christina,' he said. 'I promise! Our new cousins look like fun! Alice and Barbara, I'm pleased to meet you.'

'Go and eat your breakfast,' Christina said. 'Next time we see you, I hope you will look a great deal tidier than that,' and Hay disappeared into the dining room to join his brothers, with a cheeky grin. 'Of course, he is a great favourite,' Christina sighed and promised to meet them at the foot of the stairs in half an hour, when it would be time to leave. 'It's only ten minutes across the Voe to Olnafirth Kirk,' she smiled, 'and it is such a lovely day that it should be a delightful trip.'

Back up in her attic, Barbara went over to the window, and what she saw seemed quite different by day. From so high up she could see right over the tops of the trees in the glade. She could even see the roofs of the summer-house and the dovecote, small and pointed and tiled with the same slates as the Big House, as if to show how important they were.

Then, over to the left, was the jetty she had stepped on to last night, private no doubt to Busta House. Several rowing-boats lay peacefully in the calm water beside it, and a little knot of men had gathered. Mr Fisken

51

joined them, towering above Mr Gifford and the other men who were there obviously to row the boats.

She decided the white lace shawl that Aunt Ellice had knitted would be light and warm enough, and pretty enough for the Kirk. She shook it out of its white canvas bag, and then out of its black paper, pleased to see that it was not creased at all, but sparkling white from the sulphur Aunt Mary had smoked it in, with every point well stretched out, just as it had come off the stretching board. It was supposed to look like a cobweb. She thought it almost did, and so did Alice's when they went back downstairs again.

'Oh, what very pretty shawls!' Christina greeted them. 'Those patterns are quite new to me. You must show me how to knit them.'

'Alice will show you, Miss Christina. She is a much better knitter than I am,' Barbara assured her quickly, still worried about Alice's place in this house, because if Alice could not settle down happily here, then they would both have to go back home. And she herself didn't want to go back to Lerwick. There were so many interesting people here in Busta House.

Then they set off, lifting their skirts over the rough path down to the jetty. Mr Gifford directed them into the boats, handing all three ladies into the first one with great decorum, and settling them carefully under the rugs.

'Even on a beautiful day like this, it can still

52

be cold on the water,' he fussed, as Mr Fisken stepped in along with them and sat down facing Barbara.

This gave her a perfect excuse to study him in detail, and she liked what she saw, from his large frame right up to his high forehead above his huge brown eyes. She had first noticed his eyes in the dining room, had thought about them afterwards and decided she was mistaken. No human eyes could be as large and as liquid as those. But they were, after all, and full of kindness.

When three of the Gifford sons came running their father tut-tutted, inspected them carefully and finally allowed them to board the second boat. At the last moment John Gifford walked casually down to the pier, wearing his hat and carrying his silver-topped cane. Barbara regarded him with the liveliest interest, and saw today that where the other Giffords were fair and open-faced, he was the opposite, his face closed in and darkly secretive. And he was as devastatingly attractive as she had found him at first sight. The eyes that met hers as she stared at him really were smoky, smudgy, smouldering grey eyes, infinitely exciting.

But John Gifford did not give her a second glance as the boats glided away, and Barbara looked about her, feeling very snubbed. The water was too blue, the rocks too cruel, and in this hard northern light the grass too green, brilliantly green. She realised they were out in the open Voe in almost the same waters as yesterday when she thought the end of her life had come, and suddenly everything living was too real, right down to Mr Gifford's polished and neatly trimmed nails as he tucked in the rugs more firmly.

'It's all right, Miss Barbara,' John Fisken whispered, as if he could read her mind, 'we turn off Busta Voe here, into Olnafirth Voe. The Kirk is just around the corner.'

Many other boats had congregated there in that quiet bay. Several people were walking towards the Kirk, and when they got there they took their seats in silence. Barbara heard nothing of John Fisken's sermon. She watched his face instead, and from time to time glanced from him to John Gifford. They were both so tall and so dark, but where John Gifford's expression was taut with ill-humour, even rebellion, John Fisken's remained composed and self-possessed.

*   *   *

Mr Thomas Gifford heard very little of the sermon, either. Too preoccupied with family worries to listen, he allowed his mind to wander. Every time he came to this Kirk he was reminded of his youngest daughter, Andrina, and the disgrace it was that she had run away and would never be married here.

He closed his eyes briefly and Andrina's face floated before him. So pretty, so young—only fifteen years old—and so rebellious with her flashing eyes and quick smile. It didn't matter how foolish she was, he adored this youngest daughter of his more than all his other children. Did she have any idea how much she had hurt her old father?

Patrick Gifford was handsome. Nobody could deny it. But he was a lazy good-for-nothing all the same, without two grey brain cells to rub together. *He* would not have been capable of manoeuvring Andrina out of Busta, of persuading her that life at her sisters' houses would give her infinitely more freedom. No! That had been his father's little plot, all along. Andrew was determined to get his claws on Busta, and Busta's money, one way or another, and obviously he hoped to do so through Andrina and Patrick.

Sitting there in his pew in Olnafirth Kirk, Thomas burned again with fury at his brother, Andrew Gifford of Ollaberry. It wasn't right to think such a thing in God's holy place, but he hated him with all his heart. Andrew had done many mean things in his life, but to take away his Andrina for the purpose of eventually tying her to that wastrel son of his, Patrick, was the meanest yet. Thomas prayed devoutly that his two other daughters would fulfil their promises to him of guarding Andrina from all harm.

*   *   *

It was in the dining room again, soft-lit now by candles in the 'simmer dim', the dusk that never properly turns to darkness in Shetland's summers, that the Pitcairn girls first set eyes on Lady Elizabeth of Busta. She walked in on her husband's arm, taller than him by a good six inches, her ample girth clothed in the most magnificent dress of royal blue silk that they had ever seen.

Barbara supposed that however such a gown had got here to these remote isles, it must be the height of London fashion, so looped up was the skirt with silver bows and with the same silver outlining the neckline. But even without this regal frame, Barbara would have realised that the one to watch in Busta was the woman inside it. Her thick, strong hair had not changed colour as had her husband's. It had remained black, dead black, without a single gleam to it. And the skin around her hard, slate-grey eyes was dark. It was easy to see where John Gifford had sprung from.

'So . . .' She nodded slightly to the new additions to her household, and even Barbara found herself quite nervous as she curtsied. As for Alice, she was shaking in every limb. 'I see you have arrived. You are quite welcome, I'm sure.'

That meant they weren't welcome, not at all, as far as Lady Elizabeth was concerned.

Barbara was quite taken aback by this lukewarm greeting, but recovered in time to hear the rest of what their hostess was saying.

'I shall see you both at ten o'clock tomorrow morning. It remains to be seen how long you stay, after that.'

'Now, now, my Betty,' Mr Gifford said reprovingly under his breath as he led her swiftly to her chair, and only after she was carefully seated did everyone else sit down.

Barbara glanced at Christina next to her, who had positioned Alice at her other side further down the table from the great lady. She smiled and shook her head slightly, as if to warn her not to antagonise her mother.

So! Christina had known all along that whatever Thomas Gifford had said and done about it, Lady Elizabeth had not wanted the Pitcairn girls at Busta! That was why Christina had tried to make amends by welcoming them herself this morning. That was why she was trying to shield Alice now. Christina had shrewdly assessed them right away. Alice could never stand up for herself, but obviously she trusted Barbara to do so.

Barbara stiffened her back which was already ramrod straight as required by Aunt Mary and Aunt Ellice, wondering if she would ever have come to Busta if she had known all this beforehand, but it was not going to develop into some kind of battle if she could help it. Already she had seen enough to know that discretion was the better part of valour here, uneasily aware that her hostess's eyes were looking at her and Alice although both their heads were bent.

Barbara lifted her eyes from her plate when the conversation became general and soon saw that Lady Elizabeth had no time for women, anyway. Men were her whole world, most especially 'my John', as she referred to her oldest son; he had fallen silent, and was almost morose, when Mr Gifford hinted that he would be sending him abroad again shortly. What on earth could be the matter with him? From all appearances he had everything money could buy, including visits abroad.

Glancing at her hostess again Barbara thought that if that lady had not felt well enough to attend the Kirk that morning, she had certainly made a swift recovery, to judge from her hearty appetite now. Barbara tackled the cold roast mutton without enthusiasm herself, making a great show of cutting off all the fat. But when she came to the lean she had no appetite for that, either. At home the Aunts grew herbs in pots on the windowsills, so that there was always plenty of mint as an accompaniment, but here at the Great House of Busta it seemed there was no such refinement of the palate.

Here, a spade was a spade, she could sense that. A man was a man, and there was no mint and no frivolity, no light-heartedness of any sort, except from young Hay who caught her eye from time to time and grinned, and from Mr Fisken, sitting next to Mr Gifford, who looked quite at ease. Barbara gained a little warmth from that, dreading the interview with Lady Elizabeth the following morning.

Busta House was proving stranger every minute, as full of undercurrents and cross-currents as any of the dangerous seas around the Shetland shores.

CHAPTER FIVE

Kitty was sent to conduct the girls to Lady Elizabeth's sitting room on Monday morning, which to Barbara's surprise was to the back of the house.

'Her Ladyship doesn't like the sea,' whispered the kitchenmaid. 'She says the sound of it keeps her awake. Oh dear,' she added as they approached the door and heard raised voices inside, 'that's her and Miss Christina going at it again, hammer and tongs. Well, don't worry, Miss Christina sometimes wins.'

'Let's wait,' Alice quavered. 'Wait until the noise dies down, at least.'

As soon as it did, Kitty knocked on the door and beat a hasty retreat. Christina opened it. 'Come away in,' she smiled. 'My mother and I have been having a little discussion, and now she has made up her mind.'

That was cleverly put, Barbara knew.

'Yes,' Lady Elizabeth said with a sniff, fixing Alice with a glare, 'my daughter seems to think she can train you to be a lady's maid. Go with her, and see that you do everything she asks.'

'Thank you, my lady,' Alice curtsied, and left the room with a triumphant Christina.

'And as for you, my girl,' Lady Elizabeth said when she and Barbara were left alone, 'after watching you closely last night, I can see that you are a different kettle of fish from your sister altogether! You will need stronger discipline. Under my supervision you will get it, I can promise you that.'

A promise? Barbara thought that was more of a threat than a promise, but she replied calmly. 'Yes, my lady?'

'You will look after my clothes, attend to my dirty linen and Mr Gifford's and empty our slops. Then, after you've cleaned this fire out each morning, you can carry up the peats for it—and be very quiet about it, in case I am still asleep next door in our bedchamber. Apart from that, there will be plenty to do in the kitchen and the rest of the house. Ruby is my housekeeper and you will take your orders from her as well as from me.'

'And by the way, you will eat in the kitchen with the rest of the servants. You will not be required to dine with the family as you did last night, except when invited. My daughter must do as she thinks fit with your sister. She appears to be quite docile.'

It was the thin edge of the wedge to separate her from Alice, Barbara thought sadly, listening politely. But even that seemed to displease Lady Elizabeth. 'Is that another new gown?' She peered at it. 'For poor relations, you both seem to have plenty of dresses.'

Ah! So now it was out in the open—poor relations!

'This is my working dress,' Barbara said evenly, daring the tears welling up in her eyes to spill over. 'Our aunts worked very hard to make new dresses for us to come here. They found the materials in trunks our father brought home from his trips at sea.'

Suddenly she had a vision of her father's brig arriving at the pier in Lerwick, of his tall, broad figure coming down the gangplank to greet them with his arms outstretched, of him hugging them both and kissing them.

'Bairns! Bairns!' he would say. 'Peerie jewels!' And then he would hold them at arm's length. 'But I've made a mistake! You cannot be my peerie lasses? They're a foot shorter than you!'

'It's us, it's us, Father!' they would shriek and laugh, and then hurry him along to 97 Commercial Street where the aunts would flutter around him and Mother would rush into his arms and kiss him a hundred times over . . . *Oh*, why *had his ship not come in, just one more time?*

'Ha!' Lady Elizabeth dismissed these memories with a snort. 'Well, you may as well begin in our bedchamber now. You know what to do.'

*   *   *

Half an hour later, having swiftly made up the Giffords' bed, tidied their room and gathered up their soiled linen, Barbara emerged into the passage with their pail of slops in her other hand.

'And what's all this?' hissed a furious voice behind her. She turned to confront a tall, commanding, middle-aged woman with dark hair and a determined expression on her plain face. 'Put down that pail at once!' she snapped.

'But Lady Elizabeth—'

'Lady Elizabeth, my foot!' the woman said. 'She's Mistress Gifford, that's all she is, and I've been doing her dirty work for years. She's been trying you out, the old bitch!'

'Oh,' Barbara giggled.

'I'm Ruby, by the way. And you're Miss—'

'Barbara.'

'Well, then. From now on, take the slops and their dirty washing out here into the corridor and I'll deal with it all, as usual. She'll never know the difference! You're only a peerie lass, not used to this kind of rough work, Miss Barbara.'

'Oh, Ruby, just call me Barbara. As far as I can make out I'll be spending a lot of time in the kitchen and taking orders from you, anyway.'

'Then come on down with me now and meet the others.'

'I know Kitty already.'

'Besides her, there's her sister Hilda. The cook's name is Merren, and outside there are two grooms and two boatmen.'

'But no parlourmaids?'

'Oh, there have been plenty of parlourmaids and lady's maids, believe me, only none of them would stay.'

'Well, we will,' Barbara laughed. 'Alice is safely under Miss Christina's wing, and as for me, I am determined to enjoy life at Busta.'

'That's the spirit, lass! And I'll help you. We all will,' promised Ruby, who in the future would prove herself worth far more than her weight in rubies.

*   *   *

That first year when Barbara and Alice were settling in, time flew past. Everything was strange and so different from life in Lerwick that it took a while to realise that John Gifford was not at home.

'What's happened to John Gifford?'

63

Barbara asked.

'His father sends him on business to Hamburg in the summer,' Ruby told her, 'and I don't think he's very good at it, either.'

Barbara shrugged her shoulders, and the season wore on with all the work attached to it. The peats were brought home for the winter firing, the hay was gathered in, and all the time Robbie and William Gifford stuck together, scarcely speaking to anyone else. Alice was always with Miss Christina who kept well away from the hay-making, because it made her cough. The horses made her cough as well, so she and Alice were never in the stables.

'They don't make me cough,' Barbara assured young Hay, and Hay was delighted to teach her to ride. So was John Fisken.

'How would you like to go off fishing in the Voe?' he asked her one evening. It was a great temptation. It was so hot, and the water was so inviting. Barbara hesitated, still afraid of Busta Voe.

'You needn't be afraid when I'm with you,' John Fisken smiled. 'We wait until it's very late, and we don't go out very far. We all have two or three lines in the water. It's called the eela, and at that time of night the fish come to us. They almost jump into the boat.'

Barbara laughed and went with them. John Fisken had told her no lies. As they floated along in a sea which seemed to be made of molten gold after the sunset, their fishing lines were forever taut with silver *sillocks*, tiny fish smaller than herrings. All too soon the eela was over, but the evening wasn't over for Hay and John Fisken. They got the fire going again in the kitchen and cleaned and floured the fish before they put them in the frying pan.

'You'll soon know when they're cooked,' John Fisken told her. He looked so earnest, and yet he looked so comical with Merren's pinafore over his black clothes that Barbara couldn't help smiling at him, and he smiled back enchantingly. 'Their tails curl up.'

The smell of the fish must have gone through the house. First, Robbie and William came down to sit at the long kitchen table. Then, Miss Christina and Alice, and soon it was a light-hearted party of young folks. For the first time, Barbara was happy at Busta House. She could hardly believe that three and a half months had gone past when John Gifford came back from Hamburg, looking no happier than when he'd gone away. It had seemed no time at all.

One night Kitty and Hilda Inkster asked Ruby's permission to take Barbara home with them.

'Go on, Ruby!' Kitty urged. 'We'll bring her back in the morning safe and sound.'

'So long as Her Majesty knows nothing about it, then . . . And Barbara, you'd better warn your sister where you're going so that she doesn't come looking for you.'

Hance and Gracie Inkster made her as welcome as their own two daughters when they arrived at the cottage. Barbara felt at home at once.

'Oh, this is just like getting out of prison!' she laughed, as they all sat in front of the fire, Hance at one side and Gracie at the other with the three girls between them on the long wooden resting chair.

Hance bent down and threw another peat on the fire. 'Oh, yes?' he teased. 'And when were you last inside?'

'And tell us,' Kitty backed up her father, 'what were you doing time for? I know! Stealing tea from the Busta kitchen?'

'Far worse than that!' Hilda joined in. 'She did Lady Elizabeth grievous bodily harm with a hat pin!'

'If only . . .' Barbara laughed, and the three girls descended into giggles while the Inksters looked on, smiling.

'Bairns, bairns,' Gracie said eventually. 'It's ten o'clock and time you were in bed. You have to get up in the morning.'

'I feel I'm putting you to so much trouble, having to make up another bed,' Barbara told her.

'Och, we won't bother with *beds* as such,' Kitty said gaily. 'We'll make up a *langbed* in the ben room. Come with us!' The girls cleared a space on the floor and rolled out a long sack filled with straw. 'Now, we lie down side by

66

side and pull some rugs over us.'

'Ay,' Hance said from the doorway, 'You'll be as snug as three bugs in a rug in there! Goodnight, lasses.'

When they left in the morning to go back to work Barbara turned round to wave goodbye to the Inksters and saw a stone dangling from the door. It was triangular, slotted through with a chain and nailed on. When she looked closer there was an 'I' carved on it.

'What's that?' she asked the two sisters.

'Oh,' Hilda shrugged. 'Father's good luck charm.'

'All the Inksters have a stone like that on their doors,' Kitty said. 'Some folk have a horseshoe for luck. We have a stone triangle.'

*　　　*　　　*

Best of all, Barbara loved being in the cosy kitchen with the maidservants on cold, dark winter afternoons. It was now November 1746, and when their work was done they took their knitting and one by one told her creepy stories about the *trows*, the peerie folk who lived in the hills and the lochs. They could put a spell on you if you didn't treat them right.

'Oh, Merren!' Barbara exclaimed. 'Do you mean to tell me that's why you leave a *brünnie* and a cup of milk in the barn last thing at night?'

'Lots of things happen we don't know

67

about,' the cook said darkly.

'Like what?'

'Like the selkies, as we call the seals. They can change into human beings, you know, and come and steal you away.'

At that the other maids fell silent and shifted uncomfortably on their chairs, while Kitty and her sister Hilda exchanged glances.

'Our Daa would never hurt a selkie,' Hilda said at last. 'He says it would be like killing a man.'

'Yes,' Kitty agreed. 'And as for their pups, all furry and white, with their beautiful big eyes—'

A knock came at the door, to startle them all. Ruby dropped her knitting and rushed to open it. 'Minna, Minna!' she said. 'Come away in! We're blithe to see you!'

At the sight of the very old woman Merren reached for the kettle singing away on the hook above the fire and prepared to make tea. Barbara noticed that when she'd got the pot warm she put in far more tea leaves than usual—certainly far more than she ever allowed for the maids.

'Ay, lasses,' old Minna said, looking around her audience. Clearly, they were hanging on her every word. 'I don't get tea very often, the price it is, so, it's aye a pleasure to come to Busta.'

'Drink up, then,' Merren said, 'and here's a slice of cake I kept back, hoping you would

68

come.'

Munching her cake with her toothless gums and swallowing her tea with gusto, Minna told them her news.

'Bairns,' she said, 'you'll never believe this, but last Wednesday night there I was, knitting by the fire as usual when—when—' she gulped.

'When what?' they breathed.

'When this eye, my right eye, fell clean out of my head and dropped onto my knitting.'

The maids gazed at Minna in horrified awe while Barbara tried not to laugh.

'And then, what did you do?' Merren whispered.

Minna knocked back the last drop of her tea triumphantly. She had got their attention. 'Picked it up and put it back in again,' she said.

Barbara could contain herself no longer. She laughed and laughed until the tears ran down her face while the other maids tried to subdue her. 'And then, could you see again?' she gasped.

'Once I got it positioned properly,' Minna declared huffily and sent Barbara a look that would have sunk a battleship. 'Who is this lassie?'

'Barbara Pitcairn, a new maid,' Ruby introduced her hastily and turned to the others. 'Drain your cups! Turn them round three times upside down. That's right, isn't it, Minna?'

'Clockwise, if you please.'

The old woman began to read their fortunes from the tea-leaves. She read Hilda's, then Merren's and Ruby's. They were all full of trivialities, things that could happen to anyone, any day. Then she took Kitty's cup in her hand and shook her head sadly.

'Nothing here, Kitty,' she said. 'As usual.'

'There's got to be *something*,' Kitty argued with her. 'I've got to have a future of *some* kind!'

'Well, I can't see it,' Minna said, and came finally to Barbara's cup and gazed into it. She gave it a tap, then another little tap, all the time seeming puzzled and uneasy.

'There's very little here,' Minna said, 'and what there is, is a long way down at the bottom of your cup. That means it could be another year before it happens.' She glanced up at her with two shrewd blue eyes, both of which Barbara was sure had never left her head.

'Before what happens?' she challenged Minna.

'How can I tell so far ahead? All I can see just now are two tall dark men—and a tear!' The fortune-teller up-ended her cup and the last drop of tea fell into the saucer. 'Be careful of those men,' she warned.

After she left the maids gathered around Kitty and tried to comfort her. 'It didn't mean anything,' Ruby assured her. 'Of course you have a future, peerie lass. Just be thankful she

70

saw nothing bad in it, or she would have told you.'

'Mine was the only bad fortune she told,' Barbara added.

'She was only getting her own back on you,' Hilda said, 'for laughing about her eye.'

'She's a lonely old woman going from door to door with her stories and her fortunes,' Ruby explained, 'and what she doesn't know she just makes up.'

'Ah, yes,' Merren sighed, 'but the strange thing is, more than half of what she says comes true.'

CHAPTER SIX

Spring came back at last, and the work of the year began.

'It's the *voar* now,' Ruby told Barbara. 'The farmworkers are out in the fields already.'

'What does that mean, Ruby—the *voar*?'

'The spring planting, lass. The corn and the barley have to be planted now. After that, the vegetables, and it won't be long after that before the peat-banks have to be flayed again.'

'Flayed?'

'The top turf must be sliced off so that the men can cut down through the pure peat.'

By the month of April the weather was positively warm in between the showers. In

May the skies were blue and everyone thought summer had come early. It was a shock to wake up one morning to a world muffled in grey chiffon, the mists swirling until noon. Early on the second morning of mist a strange drumming noise woke Barbara. She threw on her clothes and rushed down to the kitchen in time to hear the maids arriving for the day, shouting and clapping their hands. One by one they scurried in the door.

'What's that terrible noise?' she asked them.

'Wild ponies, come down from the hill. They don't like the mist. They shelter beside the house walls for some heat, and that's their favourite game—kicking up their back legs and drumming their hoofs on the walls,' Ruby told her.

'Oh,' Barbara said, heading for the door, 'in the town we never saw the little ponies.'

'And you're not going to see them out there, either!' Kitty held her back. 'All together in a herd like that, they can be vicious little things. I suppose you were going to pat them? They would snap your hand off.'

'Then why do they let children ride them?'

'Ah, well—' Merren began her day's cooking by lifting up a wooden cover in the middle of the floor and letting down a bucket which she drew up full of water, 'those are peerie foals who lost their mothers, and someone hand-reared them. Then they can be as loving and faithful as dogs.'

72

'Merren!' Barbara changed the subject for a minute. 'Is that a well? I never knew you could have a well inside a house, before.'

'It is, and I wish it was in mine, my lamb. See how pretty the water is, so clear and the very palest blue!'

'That's because it's run down from the hill, over the blue peats,' Ruby joined in, 'and speaking about the shelties, Mr Gifford got one when the children were small. They called him Hakki. Of course, that was before the smallpox. After that there was no more riding for a long time, until the Giffords who survived got their strength back.'

'Hakki's still here in the stables,' Hilda put in. 'Master Hay was the last one to ride him before he grew out of him and went on to full-sized horses. Now Hakki's kept for visiting children.'

'So we'll all stay inside until this mist lifts,' Ruby said firmly. 'As soon as it does, the ponies will be off back up the hill.'

At the height of the day, at twelve o'clock, the sun burned the mist clean away to leave the sky cloudless and azure blue again.

'Now you can come outside and watch them,' Ruby said, as the tiny shaggy horses whirled about and scampered away behind their leader, some black, some brown, some grey, some cream and some piebald with their long manes and tails streaming behind them.

'Oh! They're so pretty!' Barbara said.

73

'Yes, they are,' Mr Gifford agreed, coming into the kitchen. 'Very pretty, and so is this day now. The weather-glass has gone right up. We're in for a spell of fine weather, which is why the men have been cutting peats all morning again. Ruby, I want you to take Kitty and Miss Barbara with you and go to the peatbanks with some refreshments.'

'Yes, sir,' said Ruby, taking down three baskets from their hooks and filling them with Merren's freshly baked bannocks spread with butter, slices of cold meat wrapped up in a cloth and some little custard tarts.

'There's no *blaand* ready,' Merren wailed.

'Never mind *blaand*,' Ruby hissed behind Mr Gifford's retreating back. 'The men will have plenty to drink, if I know anything about it! Well, we won't need shawls today, lasses. Just our sun-bonnets,' and the three set off up the rough winding track to the moor, each one carrying a heavy basket as the day grew hotter and hotter and the temperature soared to dizzy, unknown heights for Shetland.

'There they are!' Kitty pointed to three long black slashes in the hillside. Not far away some horses were grazing peacefully down near the loch.

'And, what did I tell you?' Ruby asked grimly when they got nearer, 'they fortify themselves as they go along. Those are bottles of ale they've stuck all along the banks at intervals to keep cool, and as soon as they

74

reach them, they drink them. The faster we get there with some food to steady those boys up, the better.'

The first two baskets were left with the farm and estate workers at the first two banks. The men threw down their long narrow spades and sat down gratefully in the *greff* under the banks where there was some shade to eat their meal. They had been slicing down into the soft peat with these long narrow spades, called tushkars, and throwing the clods, two feet long, up and onto the banks. There they would dry in the sun and the wind until later they were raised up into little stacks to dry bone-hard and cure.

Then the three women came to the Gifford boys in the third peatbank. Robert, William, Hay and John Fisken were stripped to the waist, and Barbara smiled at them. She liked men with hairy chests. They reminded her of her own father, splashing himself at a basin of water and singing cheerfully. John Fisken's was the best. The hairs on his chest were black and silky. The Giffords', except for young Hay, whose chest was still as bare as a child's, were ginger, which didn't attract her at all.

Then up from the *greff* where he had been lying almost naked John Gifford rose up, and Barbara knew she was looking at the finest figure of a man she had ever seen or would ever see, and to make him look more powerful still his entire body, as far as she could see, was covered in dark hair.

75

'Barbara—' he stumbled towards her, grinning foolishly. 'Beautiful Barbara.' He made a grab for her. His hands were hot through her thin dress. They sent hot messages throughout Barbara's whole body without a word being spoken. But then he staggered and finally fell back into the *greff* where he lay sprawling in the peat dust.

'He's drunk again!' Robbie groaned.

'Don't pay any attention to him, Barbara,' William said anxiously.

'The truth always comes out when he's drunk,' Hay grinned, and Barbara blushed to the roots of her hair. 'And by the way, it was the truth he was speaking. You look prettier than ever under the floppy brim of that silly sun-hat.'

'We'll let him sleep it off for a while,' Robbie said sternly. 'Then I'll take him home. You girls had better go back to Busta and forget all about this.'

But Barbara didn't forget it.

How could she forget it?

It had changed her life.

She walked all the way back to Busta trembling inside, sick with excitement. Then John Gifford had been very well aware of her existence, after all. And half an hour ago he had gone further than ever.

That night her imagination ran riot. Tossing and turning in her bed she yearned to feel his hands on her again. She wondered how his lips would feel pressed against hers. She had never felt like this before, never, never. The first tiny little seed of love had been planted in her. She prayed that it could only be allowed to grow.

The following day she was dusting in the hall when she became aware that men's voices were coming from Mr Gifford's study. 'Our ships at Hillswick are making ready to sail to the Continent in this fine run of weather,' he was saying. 'They are being loaded now.'

'Father—let me go this year, *please*!' Robbie begged.

'Yes. Robbie should be learning the business, anyway,' John said, sounding relieved at a possible way out of it for himself.

'Oh, I've thought of all that! I hope to see all my sons in the business some day! John, you will go as usual to Hamburg in the *Sibella*. You, Robbie, will sail with Captain Francis Bull to Oporto for your first venture abroad. You may both of you go and pack your bags today. The ships will sail at high tide tomorrow midday.'

'Oh, thank you, Father!' Robbie answered enthusiastically, but there was no reply from John.

'Cheer up, John,' his father chided him. 'You'll be back in a couple of months—three months at the outside.'

Three months!

With those two chilling words Thomas Gifford killed the tiny plant of love inside

Barbara. It could never survive three months, she thought, creeping away miserably. She would have lost heart completely if she'd overhead John's conversation with his mother later that night, but mercifully, she didn't.

'You're leaving tomorrow, then?' Lady Elizabeth smiled at her favourite son.

'And still unmarried, Mother,' he said, his face hard. 'I am a man of nearly thirty. I am not living a natural life.'

'How many young ladies have I introduced to you? It is not my fault that you rejected them all.'

'I don't intend to marry a woman I don't even like.'

'Is there a woman you *do* like?' she sneered.

'Perhaps pretty Barbara Pit—'

'A *kitchenmaid*! No, I will not hear of it. Never!'

Clearly she couldn't hold John back much longer, so she had better find him a suitable wife by the time he came back from abroad. Otherwise, God knew what sort of unsuitable union he would make.

Next day, bright and early, Barbara watched Mr Gifford riding away to Hillswick with John and Robbie. She hadn't even been given the chance to say goodbye, she thought sadly.

*   *   *

They raised up the peats into little piles so that

the sun and the wind would dry them and harden them. They gathered them off the hill in kishies, transferred them to the waiting carts and took them home for the year's firing.

Barbara could dredge up very little interest even when she watched the men expertly building the peats into stacks and covering them with turf to withstand the winter weather. She was still moping when it came to the haymaking, and one day at the end of July she was taken by surprise when Mr Gifford told her that Mr Peter Gifford of Wethersta and his family were coming for the evening meal, and invited her to join the family. Why, she wondered? But she would not have been surprised to learn that Mr Gifford had overruled his wife on the matter.

'It is time we had Peter and his brood up here for a visit,' he told Lady Elizabeth. 'They will cheer us up, now when we are missing John and Robbie so much.'

'Yes,' she sighed. 'Well, thank God they all like chicken. I'll get Merren to roast two hens.'

'Two hens, between fourteen people, Betty? Oh, I think you'd better make it three, at least.'

'And where are you getting the fourteen people from, may I ask? There's seven of the Wetherstas, two of us, William and Hay, Christina and that Alice—by my reckoning that makes thirteen.'

'Thirteen is a very unlucky number, Betty,

and a very unwise one with our boys so far from home as well!' he snapped. 'Barbara will also attend the meal, otherwise Peter will wonder why one sister is there and not the other! There are no such divisions in his family,' Thomas Gifford gathered momentum. 'A very fine soul, is Peter, and one I have always counted on in the Gifford family. Not like my own brother, Andrew,' he added fiercely, before he fell to brooding.

Lady Elizabeth knew exactly what he was brooding about and thanked God that at least he didn't know that there was a much larger problem looming, nearer to home. He was comparing his bluff, hearty cousin with his terrible brother again. Peter never begged for money, like Andrew did. Peter always seemed to manage splendidly, in spite of his large family. It didn't occur to her to wonder just how, exactly. She had more important matters to think about, such as how to squash this Barbara Pitcairn for ever.

'Very well, then,' she conceded. 'Three hens it will be. When are they coming, so that I can warn Merren?'

'I'll ask them for the day after tomorrow—and I'll invite Barbara myself.'

*   *   *

Even if it had never occurred to either of his parents, or to any of his brothers either, to

80

wonder how Uncle Peter made such a handsome living, it had often occurred to young Hay, who was a very inquisitive boy. With his inquiring mind he spent his time finding out things, although once he'd found them out he hugged them to himself and said nothing. They were secrets, and Hay dearly loved secrets.

'I'm going to ride down to Wethersta,' he told William one evening. 'Are you coming with me?'

'I can't. I'm skint. I drank too much and gambled too much the last time.'

'Oh, come on! I'm not going in. I'm just going to watch the goings-on.'

'You must be mad,' William said, shifting himself on one of the sofas in the Long Room to find a more comfortable position to read his book. 'Going all the way down there, and then not going in! No. I can't be bothered.'

Not in the least put off, Hay went himself to watch Uncle Peter's house. He had become very curious, and the more he turned it over in his mind the whole thing became curiouser and curiouser by the minute. The last few times they had all been at Wethersta playing cards, he had noticed that Uncle Peter never joined in, but was always going out and then coming back inside at intervals. Where did he go? And what for?

Hay found himself a rock to hide behind, down below the house. From there he could

81

see both the house and the sea. As soon as it began to get dark the folk from round about came in a steady stream and none of them left again without a bottle or even a keg. The hairs on the back of Hay's neck began to positively prickle when he realised that his Uncle Peter was selling liquor. But how did he have so much, and where did it come from?

After that, he often went on this interesting new mission and one night, six weeks earlier, a ship had sneaked in and anchored offshore, not far from his hiding place.

A young woman was rowed to shore first, dressed all in black. Hay recognised her as Freya, who sometimes stayed at Wethersta. Of course, he knew all about her, as they all did. Uncle Peter and his family had found her crying and penniless in the streets of Lerwick one Christmas Eve when they had been there to buy presents for each other. It was more than their large hearts could bear.

They took Freya home to Wethersta with them, and Uncle Peter had sent his daughters up to the attics to raid the trunks full of his dead wife's gowns. They were all black. Even her shawls had been black because there was always someone to mourn. Hay had to admit that Freya's blonde beauty was enhanced, dressed all in black. Anyway, she had kept on going back and forth to Wethersta ever since.

So this was how she came and went so mysteriously! He was near enough to hear the man who rowed the boat speak.

'I'll be back with more of the same in two months, if you must go back to Lerwick again.'

'Arne,' she said, 'I must work.'

'No, you do not. A hundred times I've asked you to come back to Norway with me. There's a home there waiting for you.'

'Perhaps next time, Arne.'

As soon as she disappeared inside the house Peter Gifford and his family came out and formed a chain-gang to the shed at the side of the house while the cargo was shipped ashore.

'My God!' Hay laughed to himself delightedly. It was the best joke for years. 'Uncle Peter's a smuggler! And right under Father's nose!'

CHAPTER SEVEN

Barbara found herself quite nervous as she dressed for the dinner party held for the Wethersta family, and when she went down to the dining room Alice, much more used to these occasions, squeezed her hand and whispered. 'You'll like Peter Gifford of Wethersta, Barbara. Everyone likes him, and his children. They laugh a lot.'

And laugh they did. Peter with his great booming laugh infected everyone else. His sons and daughters prepared to enjoy themselves, and before long they were joking with William and Hay and gently including the girls, so that Barbara felt quite at ease. They all resembled their father, round-faced with dark hair, all except one girl who looked entirely different. They called her Freya, and she couldn't be much more than eighteen.

At first glance Freya was a very beautiful blonde, tall and slim with hard blue eyes. It was only when Barbara looked at her again, more closely, that she saw tell-tale lines running down from her nose to her mouth. They shouldn't have been there on an eighteen-year-old face, and those eyes weren't hard, they were very hurt.

Bit by bit through the conversation Barbara learned that Freya wasn't one of Peter Gifford's daughters. She was only a friend who came to stay now and then, and since she was at Wethersta for the moment they had brought her along. Nevertheless, there was some mystery there, Barbara was sure.

Mr Gifford tapped his glass and stood up to speak. 'The summer is upon us,' he said, 'and long may it last!'

'I'll drink to that,' Peter laughed and raised his glass. So did everyone else.

'I hope there will be something else to toast before it is over,' Mr Gifford went on. 'John and Robbie have written to tell us that they hope to be home by 27 August. As you all know, John will be thirty years old on the third of September, and to celebrate that occasion I am sending out many invitations for a Busta Regatta on that date. Peter, you old devil, you are the first to know! Spread the word around! So now let's be upstanding and drink another toast: to the weather, for the end of August.'

'To the weather,' they all drank.

They were seated again when Lady Elizabeth spoke, fixing her eyes firmly on Barbara for a few pointed seconds before she swept them around the table. 'Our invitations include many of the gentry,' she said. 'One in particular will be staying here. Miss Margaret Henderson of Gardie House in Bressay has been asked, especially for my John's benefit.'

So, Barbara thought dully, she has named John Gifford's future bride. I must be a fool altogether, to have had such an impossible dream.

She was too devastated to look up. If she had, she would have seen the bitter twist to Freya's mouth, and the lines on her face etched deeper.

Alice didn't mean to add to Barbara's troubles. She simply didn't know about them when she whispered urgently again in Barbara's ear before they parted company that evening.

'I am to be moved out of the attics. Miss Christina has prepared a little room for me next to hers on the first floor. Oh, Barbara! It means we can hardly be together any more!'

'We'll always be together as long as we live, wherever you are or I am, Alice. You are my dearest sister,' Barbara managed to say steadily, before she climbed the stairs up to her attic.

John Gifford must have known all about Miss Margaret Henderson of Gardie. He could even have asked her to marry him before he went away. If so, he was breathtakingly two-faced to have made approaches to someone else if not in words, then at least by his actions.

In any case, he was lost to her now, Barbara thought. Perhaps she was better off without him, after all. Of course he would marry one of the gentry. She had been a fool to presume otherwise, and her misery was complete now that Alice was being taken away from her as well. It seemed she was losing everyone. She went to her bed and cried her eyes out.

*   *   *

There was no unhappier man in the whole city of Hamburg than John Gifford, whose main preoccupation in life was women, or rather the lack of them. His only consolation was that he could visit the whorehouses every night, and very often also in the afternoons. Not that he could recall one of their faces or even their bodies ten paces down the street afterwards, for they meant nothing except as repositories for his pent-up desires.

He hated the business he was here to do in Hamburg, but he might have been able to bear it if it hadn't been for the almost daily letters from his father who was retiring from his high offices in Lerwick and settling down at Busta at last. Only today there was one, and he opened it gingerly.

Busta, 4th July, 1746

Dear John,

I have written to Mr Sympson, our Correspondent in Hamburg, and sent him the bill of lading for the *Sibella* enclosed with a copy of this letter to you and an invoice of the cargo in case you are obliged to throw it overboard. William Farquhar was back with his cargo from North Roe on the 18th ult. with only 8 barrels of herrings, 17 barrels of butter and 3 barrels of oil. He got 11,600 ling which we dried and salted, too much for his leaky boat. I resolved to send him on to Lerwick but the weather and east winds detained him here ten days.

There is no such thing as cash to be got here. Get as much cash as you can for the House Commission. Here is a trifling account of linen, more than I expected, but it is needful or else would not be demanded.

To my wife: 1 pair stays, 2 pair shoes, 2 pair gloves as last time.

To Christina: A big coat, 1 pair stays as before, 2 pairs gloves.

87

Since all civil and official offices are of short duration and I am retiring from public duties, John Craigie has been voted Steward-Depute and Chamberlain to the Earl of Morton in my place, but you have now succeeded me as a Commissioner of Supply and will sit on the Court, these duties to be taken up by you upon your safe return.

Most important for the continuance of our fishing trade, *salt*. And hard cash for the wages.

T. G.

Oh, God! John Gifford thought. His father's letters always worried him to death. How he hated the business! He was no good at it. He hated it as much as he hated his life at Busta. His mother might fuss over him as much as she liked, but he hated her most of all, although he was very careful not to show it.

In fact, he was terrified of her. She ruled him with a rod of iron when all he wanted was to live the life of a laird and do no work at all. With a woman at his side, of course, and in his bed for ever. Preferably Freya at his side and in his bed for ever. Not that he loved her. He had never loved anyone in all his life, but Freya was sympathetic and always accommodating. She had been for years.

*   *   *

On 26 August Thomas Gifford's lookouts sighted both his vessels coming into the refuge of Lerwick harbour after their long haul from the Continent and sent word to the Laird of Busta that they would sail again the following day north to his depot at Hillswick.

'They'll be on time,' he announced triumphantly. 'We must all go to meet them! Everyone who can ride must ride to Hillswick tomorrow! What a happy, happy day!'

Lady Elizabeth issued her orders to Merren for three hens to be roasted with oatmeal stuffing, a leg of lamb, apples to be stewed and plenty of custard to pour over them, while William and Hay, Mr Fisken and Barbara and the two grooms all mounted their horses at the crack of dawn on a beautiful day and set off after Mr Gifford.

Fortunately his mare, Betty, was a sensible horse. She picked her way carefully over the rough pathways. The Gifford household followed slowly behind, which was just as well for Barbara. She had never been on such a long ride before.

But even so, they arrived at Hillswick, at the head of the long voe of Ura Firth, hours before the ships could possibly get there. Mr Gifford entered into a long discussion with his agent. The other men lay around on the grass bored and sleepy.

'Miss Barbara,' Mr Fisken said, 'are you still

able to ride on with me to see some of the wonders of Shetland? They are only around that headland.'

She looked at William and Hay stretched out on the grass; even Hay only gave her a limp wave of his hand; and at the grooms dozing beside the horses a little distance away, and laughed.

'I'm not tired at all, Mr Fisken. Nothing would please me more.'

'Then let us turn our backs on Ura Firth and go on to the next voe, Sand Wick. Don't worry, we'll be there very shortly.'

She expected that, since the land masses were so narrow and the long fingers of the sea between them so many and so beautiful. The sun was radiant in a blue sky now, the light so luminous and the grass so fresh and green that they rode on in silence, happy together in what seemed a bright new world never before trodden by human foot. All that could be heard in the soft breeze was the sigh of the sea and the calls of the birds constantly wheeling and diving.

'Here we are! This is Sand Wick,' Mr Fisken said minutes later, reining his horse.

Barbara stopped and looked out over the vast expanse of sea which had come into view. A huge black rock rose out of it with a hole right through the middle of it, like a giant doorway. 'What's that?' she asked.

'That's the first wonder. It's really a small

island called the Dore Holm. It's seventy feet wide and as you see, its doorway is high enough to allow a tall ship under full sail to pass through. It shows you the force of the seas around here, to make such a huge hole in such a mass of rock.'

They rode on slowly southwards until Barbara drew in her breath sharply again, in awe. Out of the water rose a row of narrow rocks a hundred feet tall.

'Some people say they resemble the sails of a great ship,' Mr Fisken told her.

'They're more like a row of some giant's teeth!' she laughed. 'See! They're smiling on the glassy sea far beneath them, or at the brilliant sky above them, and the sun has turned them red!'

'They're called The Drongs,' he said, smiling, and gave her time to gaze at them in wonder. 'And, we're not finished yet!'

He led her on for a while over velvety turf as they rounded the little peninsula and headed back north for Hillswick again. Then suddenly he dismounted.

'Let me help you down here, Miss Barbara,' he said, holding out his arms.

She slid into them, surprised at their strength. It gave her a great sense of security, and something more than that. Nobody else from Busta was as sure and steadfast as he felt. She hoped he would become her friend.

More huge rocks rose out of the sea on their

91

left. 'Another gateway,' he said. 'Of course you know that here in Shetland a gate is called a *grind*. That one is the Grind of Navir because it is the gateway to a huge cave, but we are not going down to the cliffs to see it. We'll go inland instead. I want you to be very careful. It's very beautiful here—beautiful, but dangerous. Hold on to me.'

He put his arm around her shoulders and they turned their backs to the sea and walked on. 'Hold on,' he repeated, and she put her arm around his waist and held on tight until they came to a halt. 'There are two holes in the ground here, Miss Barbara, but they are no ordinary holes. They are the Holes of Scraada, as big as quarries and very deep. We can walk between them and look down.'

They came to the first one. She looked down and saw the sea far, far below. 'How can it possibly be the sea away up here?' she asked. 'The sea's such a long way away.'

'That huge cave at the Grind of Navir runs into a long, long tunnel. The tunnel continues underground to the next hole. In the winter it becomes a blow-hole. When a heavy sea rushes in, the waves are thrown up in the air here, sometimes with such force that large rocks are blown up too. Come, we'll go over and see it.'

Its sides were so steep and blackened with sea-salt that Barbara was almost afraid to look down. Seeing that, John Fisken pulled her down to lie flat on her stomach beside him.

'It's safer like this,' he said, and kept a tight grip on her. 'Now tell me, what do you see?'

But Barbara was silent, locked in one of her strange trances again.

Or was it a dream?

*   *   *

She knew she was really lying on the grass alongside Mr Fisken, but somehow she was down there with him on the beach at the entrance to the Grind of Navir.

'We can go in here,' he said. 'It's not just a cave. It's a tunnel.' Then, as in the way of dreams, they were swimming.

'Oh, look!' Barbara said. 'It's all rosy pink! And so beautiful!'

They swam on, exploring this new place, looking up at the red soaring pinnacles of a majestic palace under the sea. They swam to the very end where the surf threw up onto the rocks on a little beach. Through a hole in the roof far, far above there was the light of the sun and the screaming of the kittiwakes, wheeling and diving.

'Is there anywhere in the world up there or down here safer than this?' she asked him, and the next time she looked they were surrounded by seal-babies, white and furry, playing on the beach.

'Nowhere.'

No, nowhere safer for a nursery, Barbara

thought, and suddenly she was consumed with the strongest emotion she had ever felt. She longed, she burned to hold one of those tiny creatures in her arms, to kiss its liquid, haunting eyes—so like its father's. It was all she ever wanted, and overcome by so strong a desire, she fainted.

*   *   *

At first John Fisken didn't notice what was happening to Barbara at the holes of Scraada. When he did, he thought she was in the grip of vertigo, dizzy at looking down from such a great height. Her face was ashen and her body seemed to have frozen stiff.

'Miss Barbara, Miss Barbara!' he cried in concern, pulling her up, rubbing her cheeks and her hands until the blood came back to them, and she smiled at him again. 'Where were you?' he asked. 'Where have you been?'

'I haven't been there yet,' she told him, 'but I know I will be some day in the future. You see, I had a dream . . .'

She could have bitten her tongue out. What on earth must he think of her? If John Fisken turned out to be her friend, she mustn't let him think she was strange. She said no more.

John Fisken seemed to understand that she would have told him about it if she could.

'Was it only a dream, I wonder?' he smiled, and kept his arm about her until they got back to the horses. He lifted her up into the saddle again and kept talking to her while they rode back to Hillswick.

Colour rushed back into Barbara's cheeks as the dream receded. She shouldn't have told anyone about such a shameful hallucination, John Fisken least of all. But she came to its correct interpretation, just the same. She was ready for a man's love. She was ready to have his babies.

And John Fisken was a minister of the Gospel. Quite the wrong man for her dreams.

She didn't understand herself at all.

'I've been here with the Giffords before,' Mr Fisken said. 'It's quite a performance until they get all the freight unloaded and into the agent's sheds. Then all the manifests are checked and double-checked.'

'What's in the freight?' Barbara asked, watching as other men came to lend a hand.

'First and foremost, precious, hoarded tea for Lady Elizabeth!' he laughed. 'The Laird's "waters"—in other words, his brandy—and his "smoaking" tobacco. Sugar, of course, and most important of all, salt, to cure the fish with. Lines and hooks and all the other things for the fishing. The ladies will have demanded clothing, but what Thomas Gifford will want above everything else are his "baggs of hard cash", as he calls them.'

'Then everyone will be paid their wages,' Barbara said hopefully.

95

'I suppose so. Everyone, that is, except me. You see, I am not an ordained minister, although I carry out all the duties of one. So the Giffords give me bed and board, and that's all. I am a very poor man, Miss Barbara.'

'A man who is very hard done by, Mr Fisken,' she said indignantly.

'Well,' he smiled his slow, charming smile, 'Mr Gifford, John and Robbie will have to stay here for the rest of the day to see to the freight. All we have to do is greet the wanderers, and then we can take one of the grooms and go back to Busta.'

There was still one tiny spark of hope in Barbara's heart when the dreaded moment arrived and she came face to face with John Gifford once more. But that was swiftly doused. He nodded at her curtly before he turned his back on her. But he managed to say a few grim words to John Fisken . . . Very few.

'What's the matter with him now?' she asked on the way back.

'Oh, it was a disastrous trip. He hated every minute of it.'

Well, it served him right, Barbara thought, and found to her great relief and delight that she didn't care a fig.

CHAPTER EIGHT

The third day of September dawned mellow and fair, with just enough wind to ruffle Busta Voe.

Mr Gifford studied the sky. 'The wind will get up from the south-west,' he said. 'It's a perfect day for the races.'

Boatloads of people started to arrive. The men crowded around the pier and the boat-shed, wearing long sea-boots and waterproofs. Families trooped along both sides of the Voe and arranged themselves where they thought they would get the best view, carrying picnic baskets and determined to enjoy this great day out. The sun shone over the babble of voices and laughter in this quiet place to give it an air of excitement, even carnival.

In the kitchen of Busta House the atmosphere was feverish. Kitty and Hilda had set the long dining table hours ago for more people than it could possibly seat.

'They'll come in batches,' Ruby said calmly. 'The men will want to see the end of this race or that one.' She turned to James Sinclair and Eddie Leask, the two grooms. 'Now then, you two, come upstairs with me and I'll show you the tables to carry down. Then you can go back up for the chairs. This dining table will never do for all the mistress's guests even if only in batches. We'll have to put the overflow on the lawn.'

Barbara rushed up and down from the linen closet with tablecloths for them, anchoring them down with the china, for now the wind was freshening just as Mr Gifford had predicted. One of her trips had to be aborted when Lady Elizabeth opened the door of her sitting room and led out an assortment of female guests.

'Such a glorious day for a Regatta, Lady Busta,' one of the middle-aged ladies simpered. 'What an honour to be invited!'

The others twittered in agreement. Lady Elizabeth inclined her head regally and began to descend the staircase with the women behind her. Barbara went back down to the hall and flattened herself against the wall to let them pass. Lady Elizabeth didn't spare her a glance. None of the other ladies looked at her, either.

But trailing along in their wake was a much younger lady. In her early thirties, Barbara judged. Tall and wispily fair, she was quite plain. Nevertheless she looked kind, and something else—clever perhaps, and certainly very aware. Instinctively, Barbara knew she was looking at Miss Margaret Henderson of Gardie whom Lady Elizabeth had chosen to be John's bride, and Miss Henderson wasn't happy at all. That was plain to see.

Her mild blue eyes met Barbara's. She

smiled, and Barbara curtsied. Then she walked on out into the sunshine while Barbara finished setting the tables and went back to the kitchen.

Merren had plates of cold beef, mutton and fish ready and covered. There were dishes heaped with boiled, shelled eggs and platters of golden roasted chickens. Barbara counted twelve of them. Fruit jellies stood in bowls up and down the table in the dining room, and right in the middle there was a large plum cake covered with sugar frosting. Back in the kitchen again fresh-baked bannocks, buttered and heaped on ashets, were at the ready, while Merren was stirring a huge, bubbling cauldron.

'No, lass,' she said. 'This is not for the gentry. This is tattie soup boiled on *reested* mutton. A cold buffet as ordered by Her Royal Highness is one thing, but men coming in off the sea are always ravenous. I *know*. My Wattie's always black *fanted* after the fishing. So this soup is for them.'

'The worst is over, Barbara,' Ruby said in the early afternoon. 'Kitty and Hilda will serve the food themselves for any other stragglers. Go and find your sister and watch a few of the races.'

Fanning herself with her sunbonnet Barbara escaped onto the hill, surprised to be joined by John Fisken. 'Aren't you racing, Mr Fisken?'

'A minister of the Gospel is considered very unlucky on a boat,' he sighed. 'Unfortunately,

99

it is also considered very unseemly for him to take part in the Regatta Dance later tonight.'

'A dance, Mr Fisken?'

'In the sail-loft above the boat-house. It is traditional.'

'Oh, I'd love to go! I love to dance,' Barbara said. 'But nobody has invited me.'

'Nobody is invited. Everyone just goes,' he told her, bowing to Lady Elizabeth and her company on the way past. Naturally, they occupied the spot with the best view of the races. 'In the meantime let's find somewhere to sit, well away from Lady Elizabeth's beck and call.'

Down in the Voe the orange marker buoys had been set to indicate the course for the races. The yachts scudded up and down, first with the sails this way, and then with the sails that way. They made a very pretty picture, but after half an hour of it Barbara was thoroughly bored. She glanced sideways at John Fisken who was regarding her with an amused expression on his face.

'I don't understand what they are doing,' she told him. 'Do you?'

'Yes, Miss Barbara. I do.'

'Then I wish you would explain it to me!'

But before he could open his mouth they heard the excited cries of Miss Christina behind them. 'John Bruce Stewart! Why did you not let me know you were coming?'

'Because, my dear Christina,' said a

100

distinguished gentleman going grey at the temples, 'Lowrie and I could only arrange to get away together early this morning. Allow me to present my friend Lowrie Irvine, skipper of the *New Dawn* and the best fisherman in Whalsay.'

'Oh, *oh*,' Lowrie laughed and bowed to Miss Christina. 'That's a bit of an exaggeration!'

'I'm pleased to meet you at last, Lowrie. John has told me a lot about you. Neither of you two gentlemen have met Miss Alice and Miss Barbara Pitcairn, have you? They are distant relatives,' Miss Christina added while all the bowing and curtsying took place.

'No,' Lowrie said, gazing at Alice. 'I would have remembered.'

'Oh, I wish I'd known you were coming, John!' Miss Christina turned to him again. 'All the guest rooms are filled with my mother's friends from Lerwick.'

John Bruce Stewart took her arm and drew her away. 'Don't worry about that, my dear,' they heard him saying. 'After the dance I'll sleep aboard the *New Dawn* for a few hours. We'll be making an early start back to Whalsay. You know I can't leave Clementina for long.'

'Yes. Poor Clementina. How is she?'

They walked away together closely linked, arm-in-arm, his head bent down to hers and her face upturned to his, and then Barbara saw for herself why Miss Christina had never married anyone else. She was completely in love with this man, and he was with her.

John Fisken stepped into the breach. 'How are you, Lowrie, old friend?' The two men shook hands warmly, and clapped each other on the shoulder.

Barbara decided that if he was a friend of John Fisken, that was good enough for her. 'Lowrie,' she said with her usual merry twinkle, 'your arrival has just saved Alice and me from a lesson in the art of sailing races.'

'Well, well,' he smiled back. 'Since I am not racing myself today, I'll excuse you. We could all go for a walk instead. John can take your arm, Miss Barbara, and I'll take Miss Alice's,' and before Alice could protest he was whisking her off masterfully.

'You know Lowrie Irvine quite well, then, Mr Fisken?'

'Very well, and John Bruce Stewart even better, from frequent trips with the Gifford boys to the island of Whalsay. He is the Laird of Symbister there. We are always invited to stay at Symbister Hall, although Lady Symbister is very ill, sad to say. She's been ill for years.'

'Why do the Gifford boys go to Whalsay so often?'

'They go on seal-hunts and otter-hunts, you know.'

'No, I didn't know,' Barbara said with a shudder. 'Does Lowrie go with them?'

'No, Lowrie Irvine is a fisherman, and as John Bruce Stewart said, the best on the island.'

'Is he married?'

'So far Lowrie has never married.'

'But he's very good-looking and very jolly,' Barbara said. 'It's a wonder some girl hasn't snapped him up long ago.'

'Oh,' John Fisken laughed, 'Lowrie will be the one to decide that.'

An hour later, when they all met up together again, Barbara suspected that Lowrie Irvine had decided *that* already, because he was so tenderly possessive of Alice, and she was so tearfully adoring of him. But, if Alice was going to go and fall in love with someone, why did it have to be with a man who lived on an island so far away? She would be the second Pitcairn sister to have her heart broken, at that rate.

On the way back to Busta House Barbara watched as John Gifford and Margaret Henderson detached themselves from Lady Elizabeth and her contingent to go for a walk by themselves. That they did so with his mother's extreme approval was obvious from her smiles and waves and her digs in the ribs of the other ladies, who then waved brightly and falsely as well. But these two didn't walk close together, and every line of John Gifford's body language told Barbara that he would ten thousand times rather be anywhere else but here.

In the meantime, to prove that they were first-class sailors themselves, Robbie, William and Hay won the race in their particular class. Their father was hopping about on the pier in his excitement to welcome them back, and as the races finished even Barbara felt sorry.

'The yachts were so fast and so graceful,' she told John Fisken regretfully. 'I should have paid more attention.'

'Never mind, my dear,' he said kindly. 'Perhaps before the next Regatta I shall have taught you all about them.'

Then he intended to be her friend for another whole year!

'Thank you, Mr Fisken,' she said, grateful as well for his comforting arm around her shoulders, and the warmth of his body as he saw her back to the House.

For she was shivering now that the yachts had deserted the Voe. It lay quiet again and as mysterious as ever in the black and gold sunset and the cold night wind.

*   *   *

Mr Gifford was passing through the hall when they got to the front door. 'You look a little pale, Barbara,' he said, stopping in his tracks.

'She was shivering, sir,' John Fisken said. 'I hope she has not caught a cold.'

'The best cure for that is a cup of hot tea

104

and the Regatta Dance. Go and change your dress and we'll see you and Alice down here at half past seven.'

'Barbara!' Alice's voice floated out from the other attic. Perhaps for the last time, Barbara thought sadly, for there was no doubt that as soon as the celebrations were over, and all the guests had departed, Miss Christina would spirit Alice away downstairs. 'What on earth shall we wear?'

'Well, the Aunts did make dresses out of the Chinese silk, Alice.'

'I remembered them, but I couldn't find them.'

'That's because I have them, dear. They're here, in this box under my bed. Come and see.'

When Barbara lifted off the lid she drew out Alice's gown first. 'It's lovely,' she said, admiring the dark green silk embroidered with dragons of gold thread. 'Try it on.'

Alice slipped it over her head. To Barbara's amazement her sister was transformed into elegance, in a quiet, restrained way. Alice was very different now from when the gown had been made for her. For one thing she had grown up and filled out so that the gown no longer hung slack. Barbara thought she could hear Aunt Ellice saying, 'I've left plenty of room for expansion.'

And for another thing, Alice positively *glowed*. Barbara thought she knew why, but she also knew her sister well enough not to

105

comment or pry, for if Alice had a tender little love-plant growing inside her for the first time in her life, just one word out of place would kill it instantly.

Instead, she unwrapped the other gown. The aunts, with the greatest of care, had just managed to squeeze it out of the shorter length of silk, since she was so much smaller than Alice. It was rose-red and also embroidered with dragons of gold thread. Both dresses must contain some kind of Oriental magic, Barbara thought, for as soon as she put hers on she felt transformed herself, filled with a strange bravado.

With Alice beside her she arrived down in the hall at half past seven to find that the rest of the company were waiting, all except John Gifford. John Fisken's dark gaze swept over her in admiration, and he smiled encouragingly. What a kind man he was, she thought, as Alice went to stand beside Miss Christina.

'Where is John?' Lady Elizabeth said with a frown. 'It really is not good enough! Margaret, my dear,' she addressed Miss Henderson of Gardie, 'if he has a fault at all, it is that he is always late! But never mind, Robbie will escort you in the meantime. William will walk with you, Christina, and your maid. And Hay, you will come with your father and me, if you please.'

'Then that leaves me with the pleasant task

of escorting Miss Barbara,' John Fisken said firmly, and it was only then that Lady Elizabeth condescended to take any notice of her. She reeled back.

'Is not that gown a little savage?'

'In what way, my lady?'

'It is such a glowing red.'

'Well, savage it may be, Lady Elizabeth, but it exactly matches my mood,' Barbara said tranquilly, but with a dangerous sparkle in her eye.

'Now, now, Elizabeth,' Mr Gifford said. 'It is probably my fault. I was the one to tell Barbara to look lively and come to the dance tonight. She has certainly done that. In that red gown she will be the belle of the ball, I shouldn't wonder. Very nice, my dear Barbara, very nice!'

His wife sniffed, but said no more in front of the company, and the little procession moved off.

CHAPTER NINE

Little lanterns were strung all round the sail-loft and many more blazed inside. When the party from Busta House drew nearer they saw that the door was left open to light the stone staircase leading up to it. Tobacco fumes streamed out on the night air. So did the strains of fiddle music.

But inside all was gaiety and laughter, and soon Barbara was whirling around the crowded floor in a Shetland Reel, partnered by young men she had never seen before, one after the other, and all intent on fun. Mr Gifford had been right. She was enjoying herself.

She looked around for the Laird and saw that he was seated beside his wife at the top end of the loft, holding court, but that lady's eyes kept returning anxiously to the open door. They did not come alive and sparkle until the Reel was nearly over, and John Gifford came in to stand at the side looking very unhappy.

*   *   *

Half drunk already, John Gifford propped himself up against a wall of the sail-loft. It would never do if his parents found out he was the worse of drink this early in the evening.

As soon after his return from the Continent as possible, he had gone down to Wethersta alone to see Freya, but she was in Lerwick again. With many a nod and a wink Uncle Peter had given him six bottles of brandy to welcome him home. He hid them in his bedroom and every night he drank too many glasses of it, in an effort to forget his problems.

But it never worked. It made him sleep, but

when he woke up all his troubles were there again, just waiting for him—just waiting. And without doubt, the worst problem was Freya. He suspected her 'work' in Lerwick. An unmarried woman as sexually experienced as she was must be no better than she should be. But he had availed himself of her so many times, even though callously and unemotionally, that she believed he was in love with her, and kept nagging him to marry her. He was sure of the reason. She had her eye on the security of Busta, especially the money.

Of course, it was out of the question. Just imagine the consequences if his mother found out he'd married a whore! His face blanched at the very thought of it.

It was also out of the question to marry Margaret Henderson of Gardie whom his mother was trying to push down his throat. He felt no attraction towards her whatsoever. It would be condemning himself to a life of even greater dissatisfaction, and, in the end, inevitably, cheating on her.

And then, just imagine the uproar and scandal that would cause, he thought gloomily as he surveyed the crowded loft, and from time to time went outside with his brothers for a drink out of one of the barrels of beer which were rapidly emptying.

It was when he came back after one of these sojourns that he caught sight of a beautiful little creature dressed in red, and blinked once or twice. God! In shocked amazement he realised it was Barbara Pitcairn, but a Barbara Pitcairn he could never have imagined in his wildest dreams. John Gifford drew in his breath sharply and never took his eyes off her for the rest of the dance.

*　　　*　　　*

Barbara couldn't believe that John Gifford was just standing there, gaping, so rude that he didn't even ask Miss Henderson to dance, and when she had time to look around for the other Gifford brothers half-way through the night she saw that Robbie and William weren't dancing, either. Only Hay was jigging around manfully, using steps that were entirely his own. Their father's eyes were upon them, too.

'My God, Betty,' he said in his wife's ear, 'will you look at our sons standing about like a bunch of turnips! What's wrong with our boys?'

'There is nothing wrong with our boys,' she said indignantly. 'They just don't want to dance, that's all.'

'Rubbish! They're not dancing because they can't dance, more like! This is a disgraceful state of affairs! I am ashamed to have neglected such an important social aspect of their education! Well, I shall put that right at once.'

He jumped up and went to stand beside Mr
110

Troup, the fiddler, hardly able to contain himself until the little man stopped at the end of the dance. 'I must speak to you very urgently, Mr Troup.'

'Certainly, sir. Let me announce a short interval.' That done, he came back to Mr Gifford's side. 'How may I help you?'

'I understand you give dancing lessons?'

'I do indeed, and very much in demand, I'm happy to say,' Mr Troup replied, preening himself.

'In that case, I wish to engage you to come to Busta House and teach my sons. As you may have noticed, they cannot string two steps together. How long would it take?'

'It does look as though all four have two left feet at the moment, but under my expert tuition a month should do it, every afternoon and again in the evenings.'

'Of course you will have bed and board, as well as your fee. When can you come?'

Mr Troup pulled a little black book out of his rather frayed cuff with a flourish. 'Let me see . . . You understand that I shall be busy with all the Regatta Dances around Shetland?'

'Yes,' Mr Gifford said impatiently. 'But they will all be over by the end of this month surely!'

'Indeed, but I have other engagements. Two weddings, one in Lerwick and one in Scalloway.'

'Don't you have a clear month to spare at

all?' the Laird asked desperately.

'Well, I might manage to come from the first week in October to the first week in November. I *might*,' Mr Troup said doubtfully.

'I'll double your fee, sir, if so. Otherwise, could you recommend—'

'It's a bargain!' Mr Troup said swiftly. 'I shall arrive at Busta on Sunday, the fourth of October, God willing and weather permitting.'

The dance continued, and after a while Mr Gifford and his wife made a gracious exit, followed by John Fisken and Margaret Henderson, along with the guests from Lerwick, most of whom were going home the next day. As soon as they had gone the bright lanterns were all turned down low, and Mr Troup played a slow, sweet tune.

It came as a shock to Barbara when John Gifford suddenly swept her into his arms and held her very close, swaying to the music, and once he bent his head so that his cheek rested on hers. It was a feeling she remembered all too vividly from the incident on the peat-hill, when he had infected her with the germ of love. She remembered all the pain that had brought her, and resolved it would never happen again. Never . . .

She averted her face deliberately. She would not take another step on the primrose path stretching out before her, she, only a maidservant and he a gentleman laird, or would be, one day. That way led to ruin. But one by one other men claimed a dance from her, talked to her, flirted with her, and she laughed again.

Too soon the Regatta Dance was all over, and John Gifford was at her side again. They walked slowly back to Busta House, with the sail-loft far behind them, and the music and the laughter all faded away. But it was hard to shake off the dreamy mood of the last few dances, and their footsteps dragged. They were sleep-walkers parting the mother-of-pearl curtains of the long northern night, with all the sky dusky soft, merging into the shimmering sea. It felt like floating in a silvery-grey mist.

John Gifford's hand grasping hers was a throbbing, hot intrusion on her mood. Barbara felt almost invaded. Her hand quivered in his, and yet she could not pull it away. With a sinking heart she realised she didn't want to pull it away.

She was never so glad to see them as she was the next minute, when the three other Gifford brothers caught up with them. John dropped his hand immediately. Barbara smiled a little bitterly and congratulated herself on being a sensible girl. She was only a maidservant, after all.

* * *

'As long as Miss Henderson remains a guest in

our house, I want you to befriend her, Barbara, since John evidently doesn't care to,' Mr Gifford growled the morning after. 'It is a very true saying that you can lead a horse to the water, but you cannot make him drink. I do not want Miss Henderson to feel rejected or lonely. Her father is a friend of mine.'

'Of course, sir.'

'I mean from morning to night, Barbara. That means accompanying her to dinner every evening as well.'

'Yes, sir. I'll go and look for her now.'

She found Margaret Henderson knitting alone in the Long Room, and introduced herself, trying to explain how she and Alice had ever come to Busta. 'We are the poor relations, Miss Henderson. Alice has become Miss Christina's companion and I am a sort of jack-of-all trades.'

'You must call me Margaret, my dear. You see, I know who you are. My father knew your father, and I am slightly acquainted with your two aunts. It is a very short trip across the Sound from Bressay to Lerwick, where I go shopping, you know.'

'Of course it is, Margaret. Alice and I looked out over your isle of Bressay from our window at 97 Commercial Street every day of our lives.'

'I suppose Lady Elizabeth made you a maidservant with the express intention of putting you in your place?'

'She did,' Barbara laughed ruefully.

'It was the wrong place, of course. You and Alice were better born than most of the so-called Lerwick gentry here for the Regatta.'

'Our Aunts always told us so. But excuse me while I run and fetch my knitting, to do along with you. I can't just sit here and watch your hands working while mine are idle.'

'Oh!' Margaret Henderson laughed. 'I can just imagine that was how your aunts brought you up! I'll wait for you here, dear.'

'I was wondering if you knew why I was invited here myself,' she continued when Barbara got back. 'That was Lady Elizabeth's idea, as well. She has been trying to throw John and me together.'

'I'm afraid we all knew that, Margaret.'

'He is very handsome, don't you agree?'

'Yes,' Barbara sighed.

'But handsome is as handsome does, so I shall be going back home to Bressay in a few days, just the same as when I came, unimpressed.'

Margaret Henderson lifted her pale blue eyes from her knitting as she said this, and regarded the activities around the Voe head calmly.

'I'm afraid I am very ignorant about Regattas,' Barbara told her. 'What are those men doing now?'

'They will have to dry out the sails and clean out the boats before they lay them up. And if it

115

is anything like it is on Bressay there will be the endless discussions about the tactics of every race yesterday. They will go on all day.'

Barbara sat with Margaret Henderson and tried to become enthusiastic about the stocking she was knitting. In the background the other servants were clearing up after all the excitement. But although she felt the temperature of the house cool down over the next two days, Barbara found her own did not. She felt restless and edgy in the premonition that something was going to happen, and impatient with herself because she could not gauge what it was or where it was coming from, or how, or when.

It was on Friday, in the evening, that she felt the mood subtly changing. There was a renewed excitement among the Gifford brothers. As they became livelier she noticed that Lady Elizabeth frowned once or twice at the trend of their conversation throughout dinner. She did not immediately gather the ladies together to withdraw after the brandy arrived on the table. She wanted to hear more.

'My dear?' Mr Gifford raised his eyebrows at her in surprise.

With a very bad grace she led the last of the Lerwick ladies through to the Long Room, down the whole length of the graceful room to the arrangement of high-backed and lugged armchairs grouped about the fireplace. Miss Christina followed with Alice, Barbara went with Margaret Henderson, and the four young ladies disposed themselves as far away from Lady Elizabeth as possible on the various sofas.

'My brothers are going across the Voe to Wethersta tomorrow,' Miss Christina explained in a low voice. 'My mother doesn't like it when her sons are all at sea together, even on so short a trip. Especially after the incident of the seals.'

'What happened?' Margaret Henderson whispered back.

'Their boat suddenly stopped. It would not go forwards or backwards. It was as though a great hand held it fast—*and then three white seals appeared at the side of the boat.*'

'Three *white* seals, Christina? Oh, no!'

'They were seal-like creatures, anyway. And they gazed at my brothers so sadly and soulfully that Mr Fisken, who was with them, dropped on to his knees to pray. My brothers joined him, and in a few minutes the seals swam away and the boat was released.'

'Oh, Christina,' Margaret Henderson said, striking terror into Barbara's heart again, 'I never heard such an unlucky omen! They were not hunting seals at the time, I hope?'

'Seals are neither here nor there,' Lady Elizabeth said, overhearing this remark. 'There is a great deal of superstitious nonsense spoken about them. The fact remains that they must be culled from time to time. They overpopulate themselves and eat too many of our fish. And our estates depend heavily upon the fishing.'

Lady Elizabeth's chin was up. She had spoken in such an authoritative manner that there seemed no argument. The last place she expected it to come from was Margaret Henderson, whose chin was higher still and whose blue eyes were mild no longer.

'The seals are half human!' she protested. 'At home they are protected, not murdered.'

'That may be all right for a small estate such as your father's, my dear Margaret.'

'My father brought us up to believe that killing seals is very unlucky, and for three *white* ones to appear before your sons with the boat stuck fast must be a very bad omen indeed.'

'Here at Busta we are more interested in our assets than in mere superstition, and our assets include the oil and the skins of the seals we catch.'

'I don't think my father is any more superstitious than the next Shetlander, Lady Elizabeth, but I do know that he is a very Christian man,' Margaret said spiritedly. 'Also, he expects me home tomorrow. He is sending one of our sixareens for me, so if you will excuse me I should go to bed now. It will be a long trip, so I will be up early. I bid you all Goodnight.'

*   *   *

The following morning, that glorious Saturday morning of 10 September when all the earth seemed to be floating in seas of molten gold, Mr Gifford, Miss Christina, Alice and Barbara escorted Margaret Henderson down to the large boat her father had sent from Gardie and waved to her as she went away.

The *mareel* appeared on the sea, sparkling like diamonds.

'What is the *mareel*, really?' Barbara asked. 'Why does it come only now and again?'

'The sea fire?' Mr Gifford smiled. 'It is caused by tiny sea creatures. Look, they are sticking to the sailors' oars! Watch how it glitters when they raise them for the next stroke.'

'It's beautiful. Everything is so beautiful at Busta,' Barbara said with a sigh, wondering why some people here had to spoil it by making life so ugly, for themselves and for each other.

*   *   *

'Kitty, kitty, kitty! Come, peerie kitty!'

Kitty was upstairs that evening turning down the beds. It was her last duty for the day, one that she never undertook unless the Giffords were all either downstairs, or out.

She knew Lady Elizabeth, Miss Christina and Alice were in the Long Room, and the

119

Gifford boys were still in the dining room talking to their father and no doubt drinking a glass of port or brandy with him. She'd heard their voices when she passed the door.

Yet there it was again, that sickening masculine falsetto voice calling a cat.

'Kitty, kitty, kitty! Come now, kitty!'

This time it was accompanied by a sniggering laugh. She knew that laugh. It was Master John's, and it was coming from his bedroom, the last one along that corridor. Startled, she began to shake suddenly. She had always hated John Gifford. Terrified, she turned back.

The next minute she was seized from behind, bundled into his room and flung down on his bed. A minute after that her skirts were up over her shoulders and he was lying on top of her.

'Let me go, Master John! *Please*,' she sobbed. 'I won't say anything if you let me go!'

'*Master* is right,' he sneered, his hands all over her naked flesh, 'and don't you forget it.'

'No! No!' Kitty screamed when he entered her. 'I'll tell my father! He'll kill you for this.'

'Tell your father,' he panted, 'and he's out of that cottage. Tell him, or anyone, and you Inksters will be homeless and starving. So keep quiet, little Kitty-cat—or else . . .'

When Kitty crept away brokenly John Gifford knew no shame. He hadn't meant to go so far with the girl, he thought, as he drank

120

another glass of his own personal brandy, but he was so utterly, utterly bored here at Busta with absolutely nothing to do. It was all done for him, by the servants.

Well, it was a servant's duty to keep her master comfortable, was it not? And here was pretty little Kitty to relieve his boredom for a while. Yes, he laughed to himself, he could call his little kitty any evening he chose, and nobody would be any the wiser.

CHAPTER TEN

On the first day of October winter came swiftly, cold and dreary and dark, but in Busta House they piled on the peats so that every fire glowed red, and out of the chimneys the peat-reek spiralled upwards with its familiar, comforting scent blowing in the wind.

Barbara loved being with the other servants in the cosy kitchen on these late afternoons and early evenings. They were her friends by this time. She had been in their homes and met their families.

Merren, the cook, and her husband, Wattie Erasmuson, were alone in their cottage now that their children were all grown up and scattered.

Ruby, a widow, had a fourteen-year-old daughter at home whose real name was

Robina after her father Robert, but was always called Beenie. It was her pet name. Beenie kept the house and looked after their small croft, but Ruby's greatest ambition was for Beenie to be appointed as a maidservant at Busta, so that her future would be secure.

'Then I would die happy,' she would sigh.

Kitty, the dark sister, and Hilda the blonde sister lived with their parents in the largest fisherman's cottage in the district.

Barbara became fond of them all and there was no doubt that they liked her, especially Ruby, who could make up the most plausible story without batting an eyelid to cover up for her if she went missing out of Lady Elizabeth's eagle glare.

Usually, she went missing in the summer-house. In spite of what Mr Gifford had told Alice and her when they first arrived at Busta, Barbara had discovered one hot summer day a few months ago, when she simply had to get out into the fresh air, that nobody ever went there.

It had been cool and delightful running down through the glade at first. She noticed that all the tree trunks were mossed over as though they were in too wet a place, or perhaps because the sun and wind could not penetrate the jumbled and flattened branches. She had always thought tree trunks to be brown. It was strange that she had not noticed the moss before, but then Mr Gifford had

122

rushed them through so fast the first time.

It was all too green, and it smelled too damp, with a curious, still air of sadness, or something out of place. By the time Barbara reached the end of the path she was quite relieved to come out into the sunshine again. And there, in front of her, were the little houses whose gabled roofs she saw every time she gazed out of her window.

One was a dovecote, something she had never seen before, since only noble houses could boast of one. She admired the doves, gentle and innocent in their warm grey plumage tinged with pink and lavender, whirring softly in and out. Then she had turned her attention to the dovecote's twin, the old summer-house. She had managed to get the disused door open, and inside it was like a little house all to herself. It smelled quite clean and dry, and the two chairs and small table showed no sign of damp. There was even a wide sofa with cushions on it.

'Oh, Ruby,' she had come back with her eyes shining to confide in her, 'I've been in the summer-house! It's lovely! All it needs is for the floor to be swept and the window washed.'

'You'll be asking me for a curtain, next, for your doll's-house.'

'Oh, *yes*, Ruby!'

And Ruby had laughed and thought that there was still a trace of an innocent peerie bairn in Barbara, and made her a curtain.

But now, when it was so cold and dreary outside, the summer-house was forgotten again, and the servants were all sitting companionably by the kitchen fire that evening when Minna, the old fortune-teller, came again.

'Behave yourself this time,' Ruby gave Barbara a muttered warning along with a dig in the ribs.

This time Minna didn't go into her usual routine of impossible adventures concerning her eye or any other part of her. She drank her cup of tea and ate her slice of cake, all the while studying the five faces in front of her in an eerie silence.

'So, lasses, drain your cups and turn them around three times. There's a lot to tell you,' she sighed heavily, and with the first hint of dramatics fixed Barbara with her wise old eyes, 'and you all know better now, than to argue with anything I say.'

She began with Merren's cup. 'You're going to have a visitor, lass, one you've longed to see for many a year.'

Merren took her cup back with a puzzled expression, but said nothing.

'More hard work for you, Kitty. Nothing else now. But no news is good news. Your day will come, lassie.'

She was more forthcoming when she read Hilda's cup. 'There's wedding bells for you here,' she said. 'You'll marry very soon. You don't know him yet, but I can tell you that he'll be tall and fair, and you'll go far away with him to make your home.'

Tossing back her blonde hair Hilda opened her mouth to speak, but closed it again in a hurry, shaking with suppressed giggles.

'Ruby,' Minna said, 'there's a brightness in your cup, but it's down at the bottom. It'll be a while yet before you get your heart's desire, but you'll get it in the end.'

Then she came to Barbara's cup, and once again she was on the same trend as before. 'Those two tall dark men are here again, only now they're near the top of your cup. That means it's all going to happen soon.'

Barbara longed to ask her what, but she didn't dare. And Minna herself wasn't sure, from the way she was smacking the cup to see if she could shift the tea-leaves, still looking for clues from the pictures they made. 'They won't go away,' she said at last, 'and there's one thing I must tell you about these two dark men. You'll have to watch yourself. One is standing up tall and straight. The other is bent. But only you will know which is which.'

When at last Minna rose to go, she uttered one other warning, this time to them all. 'The Pretty Ladies are going to dance tonight. I could hear their skirts beginning to swish as I came here.'

They went to the door with her and as soon as it was opened they could hear the snaps and crackles and weird swooshes and rustlings before they saw the fantastic display.

Red curtains flickered and swayed across the heavens before brilliant green flashes darted across and fingers of blue zigzagged up from the horizon and disappeared in golden stars. They all stood in awed silence and watched the fiery energy and power of another phenomenon they didn't quite understand, to add to the existence of the Trows and the mysteries of the sea. Many times Barbara had seen the Aurora Borealis between the roofs and chimneys of Lerwick, pale, mostly as grey as smoke, but she had never seen anything as beautiful and dangerous as this.

John Fisken had once said those very words, she remembered uneasily.

'Ah!' Ruby said. 'The Merry Dancers!'

'Merry Dancers! Pretty Ladies! Northern Lights!' Minna snorted as she departed into the vividly coloured, hissing night. 'It's all the same! You know what they foretell. They're giving us a warning.'

Out of nowhere screamed the blizzard the very next day. The wind got up, howling and driving the snow from the North Pole in a blinding, suffocating fury of white until the whole countryside was buried in drifts.

'It's not a good sign, for the snow to come so early,' Mr Gifford said. 'However, it won't last. Let's hope it clears away in time for Mr Troup to get here on the fourth.'

126

When the fourth came they were back to cold, grey gloom again, but at least the wind dried up the roads and allowed Mr Troup to get to Busta House on the back of his horse, laden down with his valise on one side and his violin case on the other.

* * *

'I've asked for as many of the Wethersta bairns as Peter can spare to come up, afternoons and evenings, to swell the dancing classes,' Thomas Gifford announced on Monday, the following morning. 'Of course, all you young ones will attend: John, Robbie, William, Hay, Christina, Alice and Barbara. I shall get the two young maids, Hilda and Kitty, to come when they can as well. I want at least twelve to be present at every class.'

'Must we, Father?' John groaned.

'Certainly, you must! You especially, John, the most footless of all! I am paying Mr Troup a lot of money to teach you to dance, and I do not intend that it shall be wasted.'

'Don't worry, Father,' Christina patted his arm affectionately. 'It should be fun! Where will the classes be held?'

'Be so kind as to instruct Ruby to clear the Long Room, Christina. The first class will be held this afternoon promptly at two o'clock.'

Mr Troup was tuning his fiddle as they all trooped in, in ones and twos.

127

'Good God,' John muttered in disgust. 'Listen to that caterwauling.'

A minute later, satisfied that his strings were in tune, Mr Troup raised his bow and played the music for a lively dance. But he must have heard John's mutterings, for he smiled at him and said, 'Now then, Master John, let me see what steps you would put to that music?' He dashed away on his fiddle again, but John stood rooted to the spot, reduced to an agony of embarrassment.

The little man was undoubtedly the master here, and a hard taskmaster he turned out to be.

'The first step,' he said, turning his back on them and arching his dainty small foot. 'Do exactly as I do.' They followed him again and again. Then he turned back round and watched them critically. 'Now we'll try that to music,' he frowned, and a minute later tapped his bow on his fiddle to make them stop. 'No! No! You must listen for the *beat*!'

Next time he played slowly, emphasising the beats. '*One! Two!* and three four *five!* Now, try it again.'

Afterwards he told them to sit down. He had something to say.

'It's a strange fact of life,' he said, 'that girls are born with the innate ability to dance, while most boys are not. It is certainly the case in this company. Therefore I want the gentlemen to choose partners now, ones they think could help them.'

Like a streak of lightning John Gifford was at Barbara's side. The others paired off and the lesson went on for two hours.

'It's better,' Mr Troup said grudgingly. 'Perhaps this evening, if you all put your minds to it, it will be better still. Seven o'clock sharp!'

Barbara retreated to the kitchen, quivering and trying to look as though nothing had happened. She was going to be thrown into John Gifford's exclusive company for a whole month, when she had been trying so hard to avoid him.

At the end of the first week they had mastered all the steps of the Reel. The second week they learned more steps for more dances, and now Barbara was going to bed every night with flushed cheeks and shining eyes. When once she had fallen asleep as soon as her head hit the pillow, now she was tossing about restlessly and thinking unthinkable thoughts again. When she did fall asleep eventually it was always to dream impossible dreams. And then, every next day, John Gifford was murmuring in her ear, squeezing her hand and sending her into another delirium.

The third week Mr Troup relaxed his stern rule of no talking.

'Barbara—Barbara—' John Gifford began.

'You have learned fast, sir,' she interrupted as politely as she could.

'It was a challenge,' he said, his smoky eyes

129

burning into hers.

'Why?'

'I wanted to be able to dance with the prettiest girl here.'

Her heart swelled up and did a somersault, but she kept her head. 'You mustn't tease me, Master John. I am only your dancing partner.'

'I mean it. I watched you at the Regatta Dance. You were like a firefly. Every man's eyes were upon you. I cursed them, because I couldn't dance with you myself,' he said, pulling her to him.

The music stopped. 'Sit down!' Mr Troup commanded. 'Gentlemen,' he said strictly, 'you will please to remember The Space. There must be at least six inches between you and your partner, otherwise it is considered very unseemly. Master John, see to it!'

The following Saturday night, when Mr Gifford and his wife came to see the results of Mr Troup's endeavours so far, Lady Elizabeth noticed that her John was dancing a lot with that Barbara Pitcairn girl. However, there was no need to worry. There was plenty of space between them, which meant that John was not attracted to the creature. In her experience, men simply couldn't help themselves in that direction. Look at her own husband, after all these years! The music and the couples dancing had excited him.

'The dancing classes were a good idea, Thomas,' she said.

'Well, well, we'll leave them to it, my dear,' he said, running his hand up and down her back in a suggestive manner. 'You're tired. Let's go to bed.'

*   *   *

The fourth and last week of Mr Troup's dancing lessons went smoothly. He took his pupils through the figures of the Shetland Reel once more, then the Dashing White Sergeant and the Eightsome Reel.

'All that remains now,' he said, 'is to teach you one last dance. It started in Austria, I believe, where our soldiers learned it and brought it back to this country. For this one the partners face each other, and the gentleman puts his arm around the lady's waist. You remember the one-two-three beat? Then, let's try the waltz—six inches apart, if you please.'

Barbara was almost in John Gifford's arms, so close that it was unbearable. She longed to throw her arms around his neck.

'It is very romantic!' she smiled into his eyes.

'There is only one thing wrong with it, Barbara. These damnable six inches,' he said, steering her towards the door, out of the door and into the darkened hall. Then his arms tightened around her, his lips were on hers at last, and they were locked together in a wild

131

embrace. 'We've got to be together,' he muttered fiercely when they heard the music coming to an end. 'Promise me you'll meet me in the summer-house at half past ten tonight. Everyone will be asleep by then. *Promise me.*'

For two hours Barbara wrestled with temptation up in her attic. She looked out of the window at the wild waves on the Voe, her heart beating more wildly than they were. By half past ten the wind was howling round the chimney pots, but wind or no wind she knew she'd lost the battle when she wrapped her shawl around her white nightgown with the frills on the sleeves, tiptoed down the stairs, and ran out of the House down the Willow Walk to the summer-house.

He was there, waiting for her. He opened the door to let her in and closed it again behind her. The flame of the candle he'd placed on the little table bent sideways in the draught and nearly died, but then it burned up again more brightly still. It was like the love and longing she had tried to subdue for so long simply bursting out throughout her whole body when he tore her flimsy nightgown off her, and, pulling her down with him onto the sofa, he kissed her so passionately that she could hardly breathe.

Then it was the agony and the ecstasy of it . . .
Over and over again.

*　　　*　　　*

From then on Barbara walked on air by day and almost drowned in love by night. Her wildest dreams came true. She must be the luckiest girl in Shetland, Great Britain and the world.

The other servants wondered at her blossoming beauty, her waist whittling to a mere eighteen inches, her breasts and hips filling out to give her a perfect hourglass figure. Her eyes shone, her hair glistened and the ready smile never left her face. Completely carried away, in a world of her own, she didn't see that her friend, Kitty, was pining away.

Only Ruby worried. In fact, Ruby became suspicious.

Then one stormy night, trembling with excitement and anticipation, Barbara arrived at the summer-house to find it deserted. Shock broke over her, as icy as the booming waves of the sea, leaving her unable to think, only to feel, and she felt completely desolate.

After a long time she forced herself to realise that he wasn't coming at all. Shaking and crying she ran back through the Willow Walk to Busta, but in her heightened state of anxiety and despair the rotting, slimy branches slapped her face. Hideous arms tried to catch her as she ran and ran, it seemed for ever.

Terrified, she reached the lawns in front of the House, almost fainting in the relief of

133

escaping from a nightmare, looking over her shoulder to see if the demons were following her. She went to open the door, but the door wouldn't budge.

'Oh, God,' she thought, shuddering uncontrollably, 'please say none of this is true. Why wasn't John there to meet me? Where is he? Oh, please open the door!'

Always, John would leave the summer-house first and leave the door on the latch for her to follow five minutes later. Now, there was nothing else for it, but to knock. Then everyone would know. But which was worse: to stand here at the mercy of the night, or to face the music? And alone?

But *was* she alone? She was more terrified than ever when she heard ghostly voices.

The moon, blinking through the racing clouds, must have come out behind her when she was standing there outside. The white frill of her sleeve fell back when she lifted her arm to knock on the moonlit door John Gifford had locked against her. Then she knew she had been here before. All this had happened before . . . Or, was it still to come?

She had listened, and waited, but there had been no sound from the other side, and now that the moon had gone in again all she could see was the dim outline of the door.

All she could hear was the wind gusting and the waves pulsing in and out unceasingly. With every pulse of the waves those Voices were calling eerily, louder and louder. They were coming from the sea. She didn't understand them.

But the Voices had been calling someone who did understand, someone who did answer them, someone who did save her, after all.

*　　*　　*

There was a tiny sound. The key turned in the lock. The door opened a few inches and an arm shot out. Even before she saw his face in the light of his night lantern she knew whose arm it was. She knew it instinctively.

And she hadn't thought of him, had hardly seen him and not spoken to him for at least a month . . . John Fisken, her dear friend.

She clung to him wordlessly, conscious of nothing but pain.

CHAPTER ELEVEN

He knew the ring around the moon meant bad weather was coming, but John Gifford had paid no attention to that when, without telling anyone, he had taken one of the small rowing boats and gone to Wethersta alone that day in early November. He hadn't seen Freya for a whole month or more, and soon she would be going back to Lerwick.

135

Besides, he had finished all the brandy.

'You're no use to man or beast let alone a woman when you're drunk, John Gifford,' she told him later that night, in disgust. 'Why do you do it?'

'I don't know,' he shrugged indifferently.

'Well, I do. I know. It's because you wish you were married to me. That's true, isn't it?'

John spread his hands and shrugged again. Oh, God, he was so tired of the same old story! Freya was all right in bed, more than all right, but out of it she was just a nag.

'I'll have to go,' he said, staggering out of her room and into the living room of Wethersta House.

'Where?' Peter Gifford asked him. 'You're not going out alone in a boat in that state.'

'Young Peter and Gilbert could row me home,' he slurred.

'They could, but not in a gale of wind such as this. Have you had a look at the Voe?' Old Peter flung open the door. Down below the sea boiled and fumed around the rocks, the wind tossing the white-capped waves into the air. 'No, no, John! No sons of mine are going out on the sea tonight, either! You'll stay the night here, and we'll see what it's like in the morning.'

When the Wethersta boys took him home the following afternoon he was still feeling quite ill. Much too ill to be able to stand his parents' furious lectures about giving them a night of solid torture and worry because they didn't know where he was. But by half past ten he had recovered and was waiting in the summer-house when Barbara rushed in.

'Oh, John, I'm so glad to see you!' she said, flinging her arms around him.

No, there was never any nagging from Barbara Pitcairn, he thought. She might not possess all Freya's wiles and knowledge, but he was educating her, bit by bit.

And educate her he did, all through November, with a will. And now that Freya was back working in Lerwick, with a clear conscience.

*   *   *

Inevitably, it was Hay who discovered the lovers. He was returning home late one evening after visiting some of his young friends when he thought he saw a dim light in the summer-house. That was too much for Hay. His bloodhound nose began to twitch.

They hadn't pulled the curtain tight shut, and the candle was still burning on the table. *John, and Barbara Pitcairn!* For the first time he bitterly regretted his curiosity, for it was in the back of his mind that this spelled trouble, terrible trouble, if it came out. He didn't get over the shock of it all the next day. Perhaps he had only imagined it . . . But if not, the time to find out would be around eleven o'clock

137

tonight—and sure enough! The front door was only on the latch. It was unlocked.

Down he went through the Willow Walk, but this time, to his great disappointment, the curtain was drawn shut and the light through it was very dim, so he could see nothing. He could only hear the lovemaking going on, and for some reason that worried him more than ever. It was all much too important to keep to himself this time, and very much against his will and his wont he decided that for once in his life he had better impart this secret to Robbie and William. They would know what to do about it.

So, on the third occasion all three brothers went to spy. They had a conference about it on the way back up to Busta House.

'Christina will have to be told,' Robbie said in a worried voice.

'I've got a good mind to lock the door and lock them out,' William said angrily.

'Don't do that,' Hay begged in a whisper when they reached it. 'Don't lock it. Please think of poor Barbara.'

But the real conclusion was that all three of the brothers considered her to be the victim, and John Gifford entirely to blame.

Robbie contrived to tell his sister Christina the following day. All morning he had been hanging about outside her sitting room door pretending to look through the books in the bookcase in the corridor. He could hear the murmur of voices inside, which meant that Alice was with her.

Suddenly, the door opened, and Alice came out with dusters to shake outside the back door. She curtsied to Robbie and paused a minute when Christina called after her.

'Bring back some tea, dear, when you're in the kitchen.'

Robbie nipped in and shut the door. Christina's face went so white when he told her that he was surprised she didn't faint. But after a few minutes she rallied, boiling with anger.

'He should be horse-whipped,' she snapped, 'but do you think Father or Mother would agree? Oh no! They would lay all the blame on Barbara Pitcairn. John can do no wrong!'

Finally, Christina achieved an icy calm. 'Let me think, Robbie,' she said, and after a while, 'I want all my brothers to join me here in my sitting room at five o'clock. Please ask John Fisken to come, too. Of course,' she added hastily when they heard the rattle of cups on a tray coming nearer and nearer, 'I shall dismiss Alice for an hour on some excuse when we have our meeting. I don't want her to hear any of this.'

At five o'clock Christian seated her brothers and John Fisken in silence before she sat down herself and fixed her oldest brother with a stony glare. Robbie, William and Hay were staring at him, as well. 'You have been found out, John,' she said.

'What are you talking about?' he blustered.

'Your little exploits in the summer-house.'

They saw guilt written all over his face. Robbie took over from his sister, as much as to say what must be said next was too coarse for a lady.

'Hay actually saw you in operation,' he said scornfully. 'Then he told us. At first we wouldn't believe that you would seduce a girl brought here for Gifford protection. But William and I saw you too, with our own eyes. You can't deny it.'

'I'm sorry, Mr Fisken,' Christina looked at the minister directly. 'I don't suppose you know anything about this. Really, we wouldn't want anyone to know, but I had a purpose in asking you to be present.' John Fisken smiled sadly, and waited. 'Of course,' she went on, 'they will have to be married.'

'How can I marry her?' John Gifford burst out. 'You know what the parents would say, especially Mother! Even if I wanted to marry Barbara Pitcairn more than anything else in the world, she would not approve.'

'Far from it,' Robbie snorted.

'No,' William agreed, 'but all the same, John . . . If she's fit to bed, she's fit to wed.'

'If necessary, in secret,' Robbie added, 'but marry her you must, and as soon as possible. By this time she could be pregnant, and that would be worse than ever.'

'I knew I could trust my brothers to see the problem the same way as I did,' Christina said thankfully. 'Yes, it will have to be kept secret in the meantime, and I've seen a way to do it. I've been planning it all day. In fact, I've sent word to John Bruce Stewart in Whalsay already, to tell him that a party from Busta will be arriving at Symbister Hall.'

'When?' Hay asked, his eyes round with excitement.

'The very first fine day. So you had better be prepared, John. We'll say it's a seal-hunt. Robbie, it's your turn to stay at home, since our parents insist that one of their sons should always stay back, if we're having a seal-hunt. Besides, it will stop any suspicions they may have.'

'So who else will go?' Hay asked.

'Alice is not a good sailor. That will be my excuse for taking Barbara instead. So you and William may accompany us, Hay.'

Then Christina turned to Mr Fisken. 'I must ask you if you will do us the honour of performing the ceremony, sir? Will you come to Whalsay with us?'

Would he go to Whalsay, for Barbara's sake? If they only knew he would go to the ends of the earth for Barbara's sake . . . And now that John Gifford had shown himself to be such a coward, she would need a proper man to look after her. 'Yes,' John Fisken smiled, quietly and bitterly. 'I'll come.'

141

'Everyone knows about us,' John Gifford told a horrified Barbara later. 'Now they are forcing me to marry you. But it has to be in secret, so that my mother and father don't find out.'

'Why?' Barbara demanded. 'Is it because the whole Gifford family are ashamed of me?'

'Remember, it is not my idea. It's theirs.'

'Then, if this is your idea of proposing marriage to me, I must refuse. I have never begged you to marry me. I have never even mentioned such a thing. Besides, if you really want to marry me, you will stand up to your mother and father, and tell the truth! No, I will not marry into a family who are ashamed of me. Please go back and tell them I said so,' Barbara said, and ran out of the summer-house.

Christina sent for her the next morning. 'You are refusing to marry John?' she asked. 'I thought you loved him.'

'I do love him, Christina, but he insists the marriage would have to be in secret, and I cannot see why.'

'Dear Barbara, if all goes well you will be our sister, and that's what Robbie and William and Hay and I all want, very much, my dear,' Christina said gently. 'But we could not carry out the ceremony here. Our mother would stop it. She is so stuffed up with pride that she thinks you are not good enough for her son. She cannot see that, on the contrary, you are

142

too good for *him*.'

'Oh, Miss Christina,' Barbara wailed. 'What am I to do? I love him with all my heart!'

'Then you will come to Whalsay with us and marry him. Don't worry, Barbara, the right time will come to tell Mother and Father, you'll see.'

*   *   *

Thomas Gifford consulted his map of Shetland again. Really! Seal-hunting at this time of year! But since even Christina seemed hell-bent on it, he supposed there would be nothing wrong with a trip to Whalsay on a fine day, although he suspected it was nothing more or less than an excuse for Christina to see her John Bruce Stewart.

The thing to do was to find the shortest sea journey to Whalsay, and just as he thought, it would be from Bellister to Symbister.

The Busta party set off at first light on 8 December, riding slowly eastwards over poor, almost non-existent roads to Bellister. John Bruce Stewart had sent two boats to wait for them, and the Giffords were rowed across to Whalsay quite smoothly.

Ever since he'd got Christina's message, John Bruce Stewart had ordered fires to be lit all over the Hall, and the first fine day that dawned he sent his boats across the Voe to meet them, and saw to it that a warm meal was

143

ready for the travellers as soon as they stepped into Symbister Hall.

'You will wear your red dress,' John Gifford had ordered Barbara on their last night of guilt-ridden passion in the summer-house. Now she went with Miss Christina to change into it.

'Oh dear, Barbara!' Christina said when she saw it. 'I can easily lend you my brown one, instead.'

'This is what John wants,' Barbara said tearfully, 'and all I want is to make him happy.'

Christina said no more, and they all congregated in the drawing room of Symbister Hall. John Fisken regarded the couple in front of him, John Gifford with a face of pure defiance, Barbara almost in tears, and with a breaking heart conducted the marriage ceremony.

He wrote out the marriage certificate and set it before the two witnesses to sign.

At Symbister, Whalsay, 8th December 1747— This certifies that this day John Gifford of Busta and Barbara Pitcairn were duly married in the presence of William Gifford and Hay Gifford, his brothers,
*   by*
*   John Fisken, Minister.*
*   William Gifford, WITNESS.*
*   Hay Gifford, WITNESS.*

It had only taken a few minutes, Barbara thought, but it had changed her whole life. Now she was Mistress Gifford the younger.

John Bruce Stewart's servants produced cake and wine, and everyone drank to the health, wealth and long life and happiness of the bride and groom. Soon afterwards he disappeared from the company with Miss Christina, and shortly after that everyone went to bed.

'This is the first real bed we have ever shared, John,' Barbara said happily.

'Enjoy it while you can,' he replied, and, half an hour later, 'What have you done with the marriage certificate?'

'It is quite safe, in my reticule.'

'As soon as we get back to Busta, I want it. It will have to be got out of the House in case of prying eyes. It must be hidden.'

'Where?'

'That's for me to know.'

'You mean somewhere in Busta House?'

'No,' he laughed. 'Never!'

'Then you must mean over the sea. But I'm not going to pray, cither. You can take charge of it with my blessing, but you will not do so until I make a waterproof cover to put it in. I don't trust the sea, especially Busta Voe.'

'You're a sweet little Shetland lamb, Barbara, and I want to make another meal of you right now,' he said, rolling over her again.

Christmas came and Christmas went and then it was the New Year of 1748. The weather was atrocious. It was so bad that John Gifford didn't get down to Wethersta until the middle of March. By that time he was bored with his sweet young Shetland lamb. He was glutted with it, and longed for wilder Norwegian meat.

Like Freya . . . Until Kitty Inkster put her oar in, next.

'What the hell do *you* want?' he asked her, unable to believe his eyes when he found her waiting for him in his bedroom one evening. He thought all that was long since dead and buried.

'I'm pregnant. Six or seven months pregnant.'

'What's that got to do with me? What are you telling me for?'

'Because you're the father. You are the only man who could be. I've never been with anyone else, and you know it.'

'What do your family say? Have you told them?'

'No, and God knows how I've managed to hide it from them, especially my sister Hilda. But I can hide it no longer. Something will have to be done. What are you going to do about it?'

The shock of it numbed John Gifford's brain. Here he was, married to one woman he

146

didn't want any more, and confronted by another he scarcely even knew accusing him of being the father of her child. Something would certainly have to be done before his parents found out about the terrible mess he was in.

But what?

John Gifford looked at Kitty with loathing and disgust. 'This is only Monday,' he said. 'Come back on Friday at this time and I'll tell you what to do.'

Kitty turned away worriedly to go back to the kitchen. At the door she did her best to square herself up and smile as though nothing had happened. She could hear the chink of teacups inside and the voice of old Minna, the fortune-teller. *Thank God.* Perhaps she would give her an inkling of what would happen to her, at last.

CHAPTER TWELVE

'It's right fine to be back, lasses,' Minna sighed thankfully, drinking three cups of tea one after the other before she looked up again.

The maids waited impatiently, for already one of her previous prophecies had come to pass. After five years away in Canada, Merren Erasmuson's oldest son, Hanci, had come home unannounced to see his family and send flutters through the hearts of all the young girls. Hanci was big and broad and fair-haired, and Merren said in the kitchen of Busta that she believed he was looking around for a Shetland girl to marry and take back to Canada.

'Has he asked you yet?' Minna directed her sharp old eyes at Hilda.

Hilda dissolved into a gale of giggles, blushing to the roots of her blonde hair and shaking her head.

'He will, though, and soon. I told you that before, didn't I? And then you, Ruby, will get your heart's desire. Wait and see. Old Minna's never far wrong!'

She read Barbara's cup. 'Nothing's changed,' she said, 'except that it's all coming closer and closer. The leaves are moving up the cup. They're half-way up now. What about your cup, Kitty?' I'll read it next.'

But as soon as she took it, all the maids knew that something was very far wrong. 'No,' Minna said, 'there isn't a tea-leaf in it to read. There's nothing at all. But don't worry, Kitty, I'll lay out the cards for you instead,' and opening her bag she drew out a pack of cards and spread them in her hand. 'Pick seven, Kitty. Any seven you like.'

When she looked at the seven cards Kitty had picked she wasn't pleased with those, either, and repeated the whole performance. But it seemed the second draw was no better than the first.

'It's not working for you tonight, lass,' she said, so sadly that it sent shivers down everyone's spine. 'The only thing I can do for you now is to pick seven cards myself, on your behalf.'

The silence in the kitchen went on and on. Even Hilda had subsided and was looking at the old woman fearfully.

'No!' Minna shouted. After one look at the cards she had picked herself she threw them from her hand. 'I can't read your fortune tonight,' she told Kitty, bending down to pick up the cards from the floor. 'We'll try again next time I come.'

Kitty sat still with a face gone ashen. She seemed in a daze. Barbara was quicker than old Minna to bend down. When she picked up the cards she saw that they were all black, and none blacker than the Ace of Spades.

She knew what that meant. It meant death.

*   *   *

After the other maids left to go home, Barbara wondered where John Gifford was. She got her answer from her own totally innocent, naive sister, when she went to see her in Miss Christina's room.

'The house is quiet tonight,' Miss Christina smiled. 'My brothers have gone to Wethersta. John doesn't always go, but unfortunately—'

'He's gone to see Freya,' Alice put in.

149

'Who is Freya?' Barbara, seized the opportunity to ask.

'Her father was a Norwegian,' Christina told her. 'John Bruce Stewart told me,' and went on to tell Barbara the whole story as far as she knew it herself.

*　　*　　*

A deck-hand aboard the *Hessa*, Erik Olsen had never amounted to much, but after his wife died and left him with a fourteen-year-old daughter he was all at sea, even on dry land.

The young skipper, Arne Johansson, came to his log cabin in Sotra, an isle off Bergen, to chivvy him up. 'We've got to sail tonight, Erik, and I need all hands. Bring Freya along, if you must.'

On the trip across to Shetland Arne fell in love with the girl. In his view she was the epitome of Nordic beauty, tall for her age, slim and blonde. 'What have you decided to do with her?' he asked her father.

'I know a Mistress Thomason in Lerwick,' Erik said. 'She's old, but I've stayed with her before in her house in Hangcliffe Lane. I'll put Freya there.'

Freya hated Mistress Thomason, the cackling old witch with the button eyes.

*　　*　　*

'Freya,' Captain Arne said a year later, after he'd told her as gently as possible that her father had disappeared over the side of the *Hessa*, 'come back to Norway with me. You can stay in my house.'

But Freya didn't like Arne much, either. He was too square. Everything about him was square: his body, his chin, his face, his hands with their spatulate fingernails. Worse still, and to crown all, he always wore a square hat on top of his blonde square head. She couldn't bear him.

'I'll stay in Lerwick a while longer, sir,' she said.

'But how will you live now, without your father to support you?'

'I'll find work, Captain Johansson.'

'Well, the *Hessa* will be back in two months. I'll come and see you again then.'

Spotlessly clean and well turned out, she applied to every big house in the town. 'I can cook. I can clean. And I love children,' she begged the Lerwick matrons.

They took one look at the shining young girl and shut their doors. One glance told them there was no doubt that she was as capable as she claimed. But that same glance also told them that a beautiful young girl like that in the house would be a serious temptation for their husbands.

Her situation became more and more desperate as the Witch Thomason constantly

151

nagged at her and threatened to throw her out on the streets unless she could pay her keep. That was when, quite by chance, Uncle Peter and his family saved her. They found her crawling along Commercial Street one night of downpour at Christmas, badly knocked about. They took her home, but it took her a long time to recover.

*   *   *

'What a horrible, sad story!' Barbara said, when Miss Christina had finished it. 'Do you think she's recovered, even yet?'

'I don't think so. Every time we see her she seems more dragged down than ever. We know that she does work of some sort in Lerwick, a few months at a time. Then she always comes back to Wethersta, as if to build her strength up again. There's some mystery about Freya. What it is I don't know.'

But John Bruce Stewart hadn't told Christina the whole story, if he even knew it himself. He couldn't have known what Freya's miserable life was like with old Mistress Thomason, day after day.

'You *must* pay your way,' the old woman kept insisting.

'I'm trying, Mistress Thomason, but with no luck.'

'If I looked like you, and if I were your age,' the old woman nudged her and cackled, 'I know where I could be making a fortune. Try working at night, lass. Go down along the boats.'

So Freya had been going down along the boats and plying her trade, but she never worked the Norwegian boats, for fear that it would get back to Captain Arne. Only the Dutch, German and occasional Scottish boats were granted her favours, and she made them pay. She got enough money to rent a rat-hole of her own in Lerwick, and buy food to keep her living.

As it was, Arne kept his word and came to visit her every two months. She always had a different job, she told him, and she had made some friends at Wethersta, near Busta. What she didn't tell him was the degradation she had been sliding into until the Giffords of Wethersta had come to her rescue, and she could go with them for a period of peace, proud of herself that she could pay her way, telling Uncle Peter that he must take money for her keep or else she would never come back.

It was a coincidence that the *Hessa* came to Wethersta the following February to deliver smuggled brandy. It was the perfect way to get back to Lerwick, to her work and to the money. Everyone had to have money, she reckoned.

Two months later, which was all she could stand at a time, at the end of April she went back to Wethersta on the *Hessa*, and so a regular routine began, and continued. Each time, Arne used every argument under the sun to persuade her to go back to Norway with him and marry him, but each time she refused.

She had become heavily involved with John Gifford of Busta, instead.

In fact, she was obsessed with him.

By the time the Gifford boys did manage to get down to Wethersta Freya had gone again to Lerwick and wouldn't be back for another two months, as usual. Disappointed and frustrated, John's drinking orgies became worse, and lasted longer. His three brothers went with him, gambling and drinking the evenings away, but they, at least, were always able to get back home to their beds. More often than not, they made excuses for him.

'John's not well at all, Barbara,' Robbie told her. 'I can see as much as he will have to stay in bed at Wethersta for a couple of days, the state he's in.'

He didn't tell her that he was on a terrible binge, fighting drunk as soon as he opened his eyes, and pouring more and more brandy down his throat after that until he passed out again.

John Gifford was looking for inspiration, a solution to his problem, at the bottom of every glass, but none came. He had thought of everything, but there was no answer. Drowning was out of the question. He would never get Kitty to come down to the cliffs with him by herself. Poison? There was none in the house that he knew of. What excuse would there be for enticing her outside and then shooting her in broad daylight? Whatever he did, he would have to do it inside Busta itself, and it would have to be done shortly.

Robbie didn't need to tell Barbara that there was something wrong with John. She knew there was something very far wrong with him, but he was so secretive that she could only wait for him to tell her.

*   *   *

John Gifford came back from Wethersta looking the same as usual, but in fact he was a volcano of suppressed emotions waiting to erupt. His uncle had given him just enough brandy to steady him on to his feet, along with the advice that fresh air would finish the job, and sober him up. But it hadn't.

And it was Friday. Time had run out, and he had no idea what he was going to do. But he would have to face up to it before that girl talked. Sure enough, Kitty Inkster knocked on his bedroom door at exactly seven o'clock, an hour before she was due to go home. It was his last chance. He gulped a swig of brandy and opened the door.

'What are we going to do?' she asked, her

face set and determined.

It was the last straw. 'What are we going to do,' indeed! But with that last brandy a desperate plan came into his head.

'Be very quiet, and come with me, Kitty.'

'Where?'

'Just along to the end of the landing. There's something I want you to see down in the hall. Is anyone else about?'

'No, sir.'

'Good. I want this to be a secret between you and me. Go on ahead so that you can warn me if anyone comes.'

'What is this all about, Master John?'

'Just do as I say, little Kitty, and when you get to the stairs, lean over the banister. Then you'll see.'

Disgusted, Kitty walked on ahead. He was drunk, as usual. She only hoped that he had decided what was the right thing to do, because when she got home tonight she was going to tell—

It was the last thought Kitty Inkster had before John Gifford, using all his weight and all his force rushed at her, pushed her over the banister, and she fell to her death in the hall. Like lightning he was down the stairs and standing beside her body seconds after the crash alerted the whole House. Everybody came running. His father came out of his study, and swayed where he stood.

'Good God Almighty!' he said, his face

snow-white.

'What has happened, Thomas?' Lady Elizabeth wailed when she saw the banister in splinters and Kitty lying in the hall.

The Gifford boys stood back in shocked silence. Miss Christina and Alice stood with their hands to their mouths, while the other servants tried to stop Hilda's terrible screams.

'What happened here?' Thomas Gifford demanded. 'Does anyone know? How could she have fallen over the banister, and with such force? That banister is made of solid oak.'

'I heard a rushing sound and looked up,' John Gifford said. 'Then she crashed down at my feet.'

Nobody else spoke.

'Her parents will have to be told,' Barbara said at last, kneeling down beside her with tears running down her face. 'Oh, poor Kitty! Poor Kitty!'

'We'd better carry her home,' Robbie said. 'John, William, Hay . . .'

'No, you will not,' his father said. 'You'll leave her where she is. Ruby, get a sheet to cover her poor body. I'll go myself to break the news to the Inksters, and fetch them here. I want them to see her exactly as we found her.'

*　　　*　　　*

Later that night Hance Inkster sat by the fire

157

and sobbed. Then he rose up and went to fetch his brothers, Magnus, Simon and Peter from Grobsness, where the Inksters originated, so that the men were all sitting in the kitchen of his cottage when Hilda and her mother came through from the but end where they had been laying out Kitty's body.

Gracie sat down heavily. Lines of strain were deep on her face. 'There's worse,' she said quietly. 'We never knew that Kitty was trying to hide something from us. She had bound herself tightly. When Hilda and I undressed her, and took all the strappings off her, we saw that she must have been about six months pregnant.'

'Pregnant?' Hance asked dazedly. 'How could she be pregnant? She was never out of our sight unless with the other maids. Hilda—'

'Father,' Hilda sobbed, 'she was always with us. Somebody was always with Kitty except when she was doing her work inside Busta House.'

'Then somebody inside the House was to blame,' Gracie said.

'It wouldn't be Hay, or William or Robbie,' Hilda said firmly. 'They would never do that. They are nice boys.'

'*Nice boys . . .*' Hance smiled bitterly.

'But she hated Master John,' Hilda added with a sob.

'And did she fall, or was she pushed?' Simon Inkster asked, 'because I don't believe that

158

Kitty would deliberately take her own life, even if she was so worried and shamed.'

'None of us would do such a thing,' Peter Inkster agreed. 'It's going against the Bible.'

Then Magnus, the elder, spoke up.

'We'll never know which one was to blame,' he said calmly. 'But there must be retribution for this. An eye for an eye, brothers, and a tooth for a tooth. It says so in the Bible.'

CHAPTER THIRTEEN

By the middle of April Barbara knew there was something far wrong with herself too. She was sick every morning, very, very sick. It hindered her work. She tried getting up even earlier, but that only prolonged her helpless vomiting.

It went on for a week when Ruby, who was worried about her already, went up to the attic to find out why she hadn't come down to the kitchen that morning.

'Oh, Ruby . . .' Barbara shuddered, and vomited again. 'I feel so awful.'

'You have caught cold?'

'No.'

'Are you in pain?'

'No.'

'Oh, Barbara, my lamb . . .' Ruby held her head while she vomited again and then wiped

159

her face with a cool cloth. 'I don't like to ask you this, but what about your periods, dearie?'

'There hasn't been one since the beginning of February, Ruby.'

'Then you know what it is, what it must be. You are expecting a child. Oh, my God, my God!'

Barbara stopped being sick. A baby! John's baby! She longed to tell her friend how wonderful that made her feel. And then she realised that nobody could be told the secret of her marriage, not even Ruby. Instead, she smiled radiantly.

'Don't worry, Ruby. I don't think it's that, at all.'

'I hope not. But if so, you will be showing in another month, and then everyone will know.'

'You don't mean to get rid of it? I would never get rid of a baby!'

'Of course not, dearie. But if it comes to that, I'll come up here in the mornings and help you. You will have to be bound up as tight as we dare so that Her Majesty won't find out. If she does, you'll be out on your ear.'

'Oh, Ruby!' Barbara laughed. 'She can't do that! You see—' Once again she stopped herself betraying the secret and took Ruby's arm. 'You see, the sickness has gone away now! Let's go downstairs.'

*   *   *

'Something is troubling you, Alice?' Christina put down her knitting and looked her straight in the eye. 'I can see that there is. Well, I can't have my dearest friend in Busta worrying like this! Tell me about it.'

'It's Barbara.'

'Barbara? What about her?'

'Oh, Miss Christina, she's not well! Haven't you noticed? She looks terrible. The very shape of her face has changed.'

'Well, it's only natural, my dear, for a young married woman.'

'Oh, my God! My God! But she's not married,' Alice whispered, and then fainted where she stood.

She came round to find Christina was rubbing her hands and fanning her face anxiously. 'That was all my fault, Alice,' she said. 'I shouldn't have given you such a shock. But truly, it's all right. Barbara and John were secretly married in Whalsay on 8 December last year, but now that there's a baby on the way it won't be a secret any longer.'

Lady Elizabeth's eagle eyes were on her next, when Barbara walked the whole length of the Long Room that evening to serve wine and biscuits.

'That girl is changed,' she told her husband, not bothering to lower her voice, so that both Christina and Alice were near enough to hear it.

Alice got up and followed her sister to the

161

kitchen. 'Stay out here with me,' she said at the kitchen door. 'I want to talk to you, Barbara.'

'What is it?'

'What is it? You didn't even tell me you were married!'

'It was a secret,' Barbara smiled dreamily, 'but not now. Let me tell you first, Alice, before the whole world knows—before John himself knows. We're going to have a child.'

'Well, Lady Elizabeth suspects. I hope you can show her your marriage certificate when she confronts you.'

Barbara crumpled before Alice's eyes. 'I can't at the moment,' she said. 'John took it and hid it. I don't know where.'

'Then he'd better bring it back again, that's all I can say!' Alice said angrily and went back to Christina's side in the Long Room more anxious than ever. A few minutes later Christina said goodnight and they left to go upstairs.

'She can't prove she's married, Miss Christina.'

'She was married all right. I was there, and William and Hay. They were the witnesses, and John Fisken was the minister.'

'Your brother John hid the marriage certificate. Barbara doesn't know where.'

'Hidden the marriage certificate?' Christina said incredulously. 'Well, I'll see about that!'

*   *   *

When the uproar of Kitty's death and funeral was over, John Gifford spent a few weeks wondering how he'd managed to get away with it. Then he drifted back to boredom again, never so bored as at the prospect of going to the summer-house that particular night, but after all, he was married to Barbara Pitcairn, so he might as well avail himself of her, for want of anyone else, Freya or even Kitty Inkster.

Love was not a four-lettered word in his vocabulary. He simply didn't know the meaning of the word. Barbara was suspecting as much, waiting for him. She was always there first nowadays, she noticed. And John had never once said he loved her. But perhaps she could change all that tonight.

'Christ!' he moaned, throwing himself on the sofa with a crash. 'Has this to be my fate for the rest of my life? Out here in the summer-house?'

'I don't think so, dearest. Soon it will all change. But are you well enough, John? Are you all right?'

'I'll never be all right—not now, caught in this trap.'

'Oh yes, you will! You'll be a different man when you hear what I've got to say. You'll be happy at last,' Barbara said, winding her arms around his neck and trying to kiss his averted cheek. 'John, darling John, I've just found out

I'm going to have a baby. We're going to have a child, sweetheart. We won't have to hide our marriage from your parents any longer. Well,' she laughed, 'soon I won't be able to, anyway.'

For a long, horrible minute he lay rigid, as though paralysed. Then he cast her aside and rose up with a terrifying yell.

'*WHAT?*'

'It's true, John. I'm pregnant.'

'NOT ANOTHER ONE! You bloody, bloody little fool! Christ, I thought you knew better than to let this happen!' he shouted, punching her viciously across her jaw.

For a few minutes it was Barbara's turn to lie on the floor, dazed. She saw stars. When they cleared away she realised the awful truth about John Gifford. He didn't love her, had probably never loved her and had only been using her all this time. And what did he mean—another one?

When she got up, so did her temper. She knotted her small fists and gave him back as good as she got, raining him with blows he was too surprised to ward off.

'Pig!' she screamed. 'Rotten pig! What else did you expect after all the times you've lain with me? The great wonder is that it didn't happen long before today!'

'Well, it's never happened to Freya,' he sneered.

'*FREYA?* What do you mean, *Freya*?'

'Just what I say. It's never happened to her,

and God knows it was more than likely, a thousand times over.'

Freya . . . at Wethersta . . . Barbara remembered her eyes, so sad and tired. She looked into John Gifford's now, unable to believe how they had changed. No longer were they the smoky, smouldering eyes, full of passion, which had mesmerised her from the beginning. They were hard and grey, just like his mother's. He was just like his mother, and Barbara wondered how in Heaven's name she had ever made love with him in the first place.

'You're worse than just a filthy bastard, John Gifford,' she said, and every word was like a splinter of ice falling from her lips. 'You're a *stupid* filthy bastard. But at least I understand about poor Freya now. I know what her "work" is now! I didn't understand before, that she is a bad woman. Everyone knows that bad women don't have babies. You fool, she's proved it! As you say, with you— and no doubt with dozens of men as well as you, a thousand times over.'

'She's been a good woman for me, that's all I know. I just didn't want to marry her. I didn't want to marry you. I never wanted to be tied down to any woman.'

'I'm no longer interested in what you want. But I'll tell you what I want—never to speak to you again. I'll have my baby and he'll be all mine. Neither you nor your mother will ever get your hands on him. I hope you rot in Hell.'

* * * * *

From that moment on, Barbara never even looked at John Gifford. She didn't know what he did or where he went. She simply wasn't interested in the father of her forthcoming child.

Her bruises had almost disappeared, but still she pulled her shawl about her face when she went for her solitary walks along the side of the Voe with her heart just breaking, caught up in the age-old syndrome of the maidservant wronged by the son of the Laird.

There would be awful consequences. Without her marriage certificate she would have to answer for her disgrace on the sinners' stool in the Kirk some day. She would be pilloried in the Kirk Session. But she would never speak to John Gifford again, and now she knew that he wouldn't put himself about to bring the certificate back to her, not even to prove that his child was legitimate. She wouldn't have been surprised if he'd destroyed it.

So she told John Fisken who met her every afternoon and allowed her to cry her heart out on his shoulder. She told him the whole story. In a remarkably short space of time, after days of baring her heart and soul to him, she began to feel better. 'I don't know what I would have done without you, Mr Fisken,' she said

166

gratefully.

'Surely you know me well enough to call me John?' he asked her gently.

'I'm sorry. Not that terrible name! Don't ask me to,' she wept.

As he watched her running away John Fisken thought his own heart would surely break. How much more was there to endure in this cruel world, he wondered, and bent his head with the tears running down his face.

*   *   *

When he looked up three tall men with very white hair were standing before him.

'Salt water,' said one to the others. 'Salt water running down his race.'

'Is this the sigh, Fisk?' the second one asked. 'Are you ready yet?'

'We will take you down to your palace now. You know you are to be our King,' said the third one. 'Is it time?'

'Not yet, my dear friends,' Fisk said, standing up, even taller than they. 'But it may be soon. Any day. Any night.'

'And you will come to us? Do you promise?'

*   *   *

John Fisken came to himself with the words, 'I promise,' on his lips. The tall young men had vanished. He watched as three large white seals slithered off the rocks and swam away.

It wasn't a hallucination. Seals really could take human form and come ashore, to live unsuspected among mortals. He knew that. And then a strange, exciting thought came into his head as he walked back to Busta himself. Had he been a seal-man all along?

Was that why his friends had left the Giffords' boat alone, that last seal hunt? It wasn't because he had fallen on his knees and prayed. It had been for his protection.

And the thing that had been eluding him for years became apparent in a brilliant flash. He had no recollection of any life before Busta, of a mother or a father. All he could remember was suddenly confronting Thomas Gifford on the road to Busta House wearing a dog-collar, of being soaking wet and tired and hungry, and of being taken under the Laird's wing.

Now he knew. It had all been for a purpose. With knowledge came the strength to go on for the rest of the time he had left on earth, and by all the signs, it wasn't going to be long.

Already time itself—as measured by humans in minutes, hours, days, weeks, months and years from birth to death—was changing into the eternal where five seconds were the same as five hours or five hundred years.

*   *   *

There was an old apple tree at the bottom of the Willow Walk. On 9 May, in soft balmy weather, its blossom burst out in a froth of tiny pink rosettes. It was where Barbara met John Fisken most afternoons to go for their walks along the seashore.

They liked to sit on a large flat rock so that Barbara could rest for a while before they turned back, where without fail white seals would bob up out of the water and gaze at them with their large liquid eyes. Sometimes they even got out of the water altogether and came to lie beside them, showing no fear and uttering strange spitting and barking sounds from time to time.

'It's you they've come to see, isn't it?' she smiled. 'I think they're trying to talk to you.'

'Yes, they *are* talking to me, Barbara.'

'Do you understand them, then? What are they saying?'

'I don't understand it all yet, because it's only very recently that I began to hear their language. But they are telling me about a wonderful palace under the sea which they are guarding for their new king. Their old king died and they are waiting for their new one.'

'And what is it like, their palace?'

'From what I can make out, it's made of turquoise rocks and aquamarine crystals, and it's very beautiful.'

*   *   *

169

A tiny shudder thrilled right through Barbara. She had already been in that place. Or—she shuddered again—she was going to be in it, some time in the future.

*　　*　　*

'Oh yes,' she said out loud, 'but after all these meetings with the white seals even I can tell they have a special name for you. They call your name, don't they? I hear them barking it out when they shake their heads like that. It's a short name. What is it?'

'Fisk,' John Fisken said, watching for her reaction.

'Fisk?' But that's wonderful! As if they've changed your own name to suit their world of whisking, flashing tails! Oh, please, Mr Fisken, may I call you "Fisk" as well?'

John Fisken expelled a long breath of relief for the present situation and hope for the future. 'Dear Barbara, I should be honoured,' he said, wishing that he could only declare his love for her then and there. But she had been so badly let down, and she was so vulnerable that it was unthinkable to speak to her of love and disappoint her again, when there might be so little time left.

'Oh, Fisk! When you devote so much of your own time to me, and give me so much comfort, the honour is mine!'

170

'I would do anything in the world to make you the happy, joyful young girl you were when you first came to Busta,' he said, putting a comforting arm around her shoulders.

'Then you're half-way there already,' she told him, turning her face up to his and kissing him on his cheek. 'In a very different way from how it was with John Gifford, I love you far, far more. At last loving someone feels right. Please, Fisk, just let me go on loving you. It doesn't matter if you don't love me back.'

'I do,' he said, gathering her in his arms, while for him the world exploded around them in bursts of stardust. It was cruelly hard not to kiss her back. 'And that's why you must never forget that I'll always be with you, no matter what happens.'

CHAPTER FOURTEEN

On Friday, 13 May, James Sinclair, the head groom, quietly entered the front door of Busta House. He knew his way around the rooms leading off the hall. Thomas Gifford had given him his instructions, to bypass the kitchen and the maids if such an event ever came up. He was obeying them now, when he knocked on the study door and went straight in.

'Yes, James. What is it?' Thomas Gifford said, half rising from his chair with a face gone grey.

'I'm sorry to have to tell you the last thing you ever want to hear, sir. Ollaberry is here, looking too pleased with himself for my liking, and demanding to see you. I could send him packing—?'

'I know you could, James, and thank you,' Thomas Gifford sighed. 'But then we would never know what he is up to next, would we? To be forewarned is to be forearmed. You'd better show him in here, I suppose.'

Despising his brother more than ever, Thomas Gifford watched him sidling around the door, leering at him. No doubt he had chosen today to visit because he knew it was one of the days John had to be in Lerwick on business, and John's temper was notorious. He would have cheerfully thrown the bugger out. 'Well then, take a seat,' he said shortly, but already a nasty pain was throbbing at the side of his head. 'What do you want this time?'

'Oh, come, Thomas! Don't be like that! I don't want anything. I'm here to inquire about your health in your retirement, that's all,' Andrew Gifford smirked.

'Get on with it, you bastard.'

'I take it you are in your usual, then. And your lady wife?'

'My lady wife need not concern you.'

'But your daughter, Andrina, does . . . She has asked my permission to come and live at Ollaberry.' The pain at the side of Thomas's head intensified sharply. 'Of course,' Andrew tipped back his chair, and laughed, 'we all know why that is! She's always had her eye on Patrick.'

Patrick Gifford! That load of nothingness!

'Never!' Thomas said. 'I forbid it. Andrina will never live at Ollaberry. It's the last place on earth.'

'It's a small place, compared to the magnificent Busta,' Andrew acknowledged, clearly enjoying himself, 'but mine own, and into it I can invite anyone I choose without asking permission of the great Laird of Busta.'

'You will not invite Andrina.'

'Absolutely not . . . *for a consideration*. Name your price, brother.'

They haggled on for the next half an hour, Andrew always playing his trump card, always calling the tune, and at the end of it he left Busta delighted with himself. For as long as he could put off Andrina's passion and Patrick's, he had got himself a very satisfactory income from the Busta estate.

He left behind the Laird of Busta with an excruciating pain in his head, his heart racing and his face a hideous grey. But even in his bed, Betty was giving him no peace.

'That girl Barbara Pitcairn is either ill or pregnant,' Lady Elizabeth harped on. 'And who should know all the signs of pregnancy better than I? I wonder who she was with? James Sinclair, perhaps?'

173

'James Sinclair? Of course not. He values his position here too much.'

'Well then, Eddie Leask,' she persisted, naming the other groom.

'Don't be silly, Betty, for God's sake. Eddie's newly married, and happily married. What would he want with Barbara Pitcairn? There's probably nothing the matter with the girl. I wish you'd leave her alone, and leave me alone. I've got a dreadful headache,' Thomas Gifford groaned, trying to calm himself, lying flat out and willing the tension to leave his head, his arms, his legs, and finally his whole body.

*   *   *

On Saturday morning, 14 May, Christina primed three of her brothers as they came down for breakfast.

'Right!' she said to Alice. 'That's Robbie, William and Hay told, and they all agree.'

She was ready for John too, when at last he staggered out of bed, exhausted and bad-tempered after his horrible day yesterday doing business in Lerwick.

'It's a beautiful day, John,' she smiled.

'Is it?' he yawned.

The Voe's lying like a pond. The sun's shining,' she said, tapping the barometer on the wall, 'and the glass is high.'

'So?'

174

'So, this is the very day to go to Wethersta.' Her voice hardened. 'This is the very day *you're* going to Wethersta, John Gifford. And don't you dare come back without your marriage certificate. I understand from Robbie that's where you hid it?'

'Is it?'

Christina lost her patience with him and faced him like a dervish. 'You know it is, you brute! Why you ever had to take it away from Barbara in the first place, I shall never understand.'

'For safe keeping.'

Christina stamped her foot. 'You could have given it to me for safe keeping! But no! You had to trail it away—*over the sea*—to Wethersta! Whereabouts in Wethersta?'

'Where nobody will ever find it. Outside.'

'Outside? It will be ruined my now!'

'No, it won't. She made an oilskin cover for it.'

'Poor Barbara! She tried her best to look after it. She is far too good for you, John, and God knows she doesn't deserve the likes of you, the way you're turning out. Well, the three brothers are ready and so is John Fisken, to go across this afternoon and fetch it back. So make up your mind to it, or else Mother and Father will hear the whole sorry story from me, summer-house and all.'

'If I can find it.'

'Oh, you'll find it all right! You'd better!

The child that is coming is your legitimate heir, the heir to all Busta, and to prove it you and Barbara will have to produce that certificate,' Christina insisted.

*   *   *

Barbara was in her accustomed place under the apple blossoms, her eyes filled with their fresh pink beauty and her nostrils with their delicate scent, when John Fisken emerged from the Willow Walk.

She tried to run towards him but her legs wouldn't move. Black wings beat above her head, and there in all the glory of a summer day in Shetland she was back again in a nightmare, and this time it was deeper and blacker than ever—*as black as the Ace of Spades*.

'Fisk! Fisk!' she whispered with her face gone white.

He put his arms around her to comfort her, but when he did he felt the same black dread emanating from her.

*   *   *

So, it was coming . . .

*   *   *

'I can't walk with you today, Barbara. We are

176

all going to Wethersta with John to retrieve your marriage certificate.'

'No! Don't go! Please don't go, Fisk! It doesn't matter about the certificate.'

'Of course it matters, dear, especially now when your little child is coming.'

*   *   *

'God help her,' he prayed to the Master of the Universe as she walked with him down to the boat. They could see the men gathering at the pier. He knew what was going to happen. He knew that she would face a long, hard, lonely time from now on, before he could come back for her.

When Barbara and John Fisken walked down in silence to join them, Robbie and Christina were having a heated argument. 'You know the rule, Robbie,' she was saying. 'All four of you should not be on the sea at the same time.'

'Well, we're going to be, this time. You don't know what John's like when he gets drunk. If he digs his heels in, besides, it'll take all our combined strength to force him to look for that certificate. No, Christina, we'll all have to go with him.'

'In which boat?' she sighed.

'The fourareen.'

'If you take the sixareen I'll send for Father's grieve to go with you for the sixth oar.

177

It's a bigger, stronger boat and I would feel a little happier.'

'Why? Where are the boatmen?' Robbie asked with a smile, sensing he had won the day.

'In Lerwick, getting new sails. And you needn't smile, Robbie Gifford. I don't like any of this. However, we won't argue any more in front of John. Here he comes. Hay, run for the grieve.'

John Gifford went and sat in the bows of the fourareen as usual. Barbara felt sick at the very sight of him. Robbie laughed sardonically.

'Oh, no, Brother,' he said. 'We're taking the big boat today, and you'll have to row the same as the rest of us. So you can take off your hat and your coat, for a start.'

'And you can lay down your cane and pick up an oar,' William added.

'I know you'll be playing cards at Wethersta,' Christina tried to keep the peace while they all took their places, 'but don't drink too much. The deadline is midnight. I want you all back here, safe and sound, and sober, by twelve o'clock tonight.'

One by one the men each took an oar. Barbara could hardly bear to watch John Fisken's graceful body as he took his. There was no doubt that he seemed more at home on the sea than ever he had been on dry land. The *mareel* shimmering and sparkling on the surface of the water dazzled her eyes. It was the last thing she saw before the boat disappeared from sight . . . the *mareel*, the magic, flashing on Fisk's blade.

'We'll be back down here at midnight,' Christina told Alice.

'So will I,' Barbara said.

*   *   *

Captain Arne Johansson sailed the *Hessa* into Wethersta on the dark side of the moon, and anchored a short way offshore.

'I don't want to be long, boys,' he told his crew. 'When the moon is high it's going to light up this place far and wide.' He took Freya off in the little boat and deposited her down below the House of Wethersta. 'You haven't changed your mind, I suppose,' he sighed. 'You won't come home with me?'

'Just leave me here, Arne,' she said, 'and I'll think about it this time. To tell you the truth, I'm tired of working in Lerwick.'

'That's the first hopeful word you've ever spoken to me, Freya,' he said as he pulled the little boat back out to his ship, to begin the job of discharging her.

The Giffords were all there, she saw. Even the minister, John Fisken was there. Immediately, she became suspicious. They weren't at Wethersta just to play cards—and other games—tonight, then. What were they up to?

'Go ahead, lad,' she heard Uncle Peter saying to John Gifford, and then John went out the back door by himself while the other three Giffords stayed inside with the minister and the rest of the family.

*   *   *

It was all working out like a dream for the Inkster brothers, down at the other side of the small pier of Wethersta where the Giffords had left their boat, in the shadow of the rocks.

'Four holes, one for each of them,' Magnus said sternly.

'Who wants revenge more than I do for my Kitty's death?' Hance asked. 'And since no one can prove which Gifford was to blame, it's right and proper that they should all four pay. But don't forget—there will be six men going back over the Voe in this boat.'

'It's a pity about Mr Fisken and the grieve,' Magnus agreed. 'But now is the day and now is the hour. We may never get a chance like this again.'

'No.'

'So let's knock out the holes as quietly as we can, fill them with clods and lay the strips of wood over them to look like the planking. I reckon the boat will carry them well out into the Voe before the sea takes our revenge for us.'

'It's done,' Simon said half an hour later,

'except for the stone. You have your stone, Hance?'

'Of course. This night's work can be laid at my door, so here is the Inkster stone off it,' he said, hanging it by its chain over the stem of the Giffords' boat.

'Somehow it'll come back to you,' Magnus reassured him. 'The stones always come back when justice is done.'

CHAPTER FIFTEEN

John Gifford began his search. He had hidden the wretched certificate somewhere in the dike which ran round the back of the house to keep the sheep from straying off the hill and into the turnip field. But search as he might he couldn't find it. He searched high and low while the moon rose up in the sky, and the discharging of the *Hessa*'s cargo grew more frantic.

Then he became aware that Freya had followed him.

'What are you looking for?' she asked him.

'A small packet in a yellow oilskin,' he said, going up and down the dike ever more feverishly.

'It must be very important.'

'What makes you think that?'

'Because you're so agitated you're not even

looking properly.'

'Of course I am,' he shouted, rushing further along the dike with his back to her.

Just then the moon sent a ray to shine on the stones in front of where she was standing. She bent down and picked out a small yellow packet. Before John could turn around she had opened it.

'You haven't been looking very carefully, John Gifford. Is this it?'

'You had no business to open that!'

'Well, I did—and I read it too.'

'Oh, God . . .' he groaned. So now that she had found out, he had lost all three of his women.

'I knew something was wrong in January and February when you never came to see me,' she said, seething with rage. 'Once upon a time wild horses, never mind wild seas, wouldn't have stopped you. But now, all is explained. You were with another woman. You didn't need me.'

'Freya, they made me marry her,' he began weakly.

'And to think I've waited all these years for you to marry me! When there was always one excuse, and then another! I suppose she was pregnant? That's why you had to marry her?'

'She wasn't then. She is now . . . Freya—'

'Do you mean to tell me you were forced to marry her, and she wasn't even pregnant? Get out of my sight, you dirty liar!'

'Freya, listen to me—I don't love her. I love you.'

'What can a liar, a womaniser and a cheat know of love? I'll tell you about love! Love was years of humiliation, trying to keep myself alive while I waited for you. Thomas Gifford and his wife should hear of this! They should know what sort of "gentleman" will be their heir. They have three other sons, remember. They can easily do without the one who shamed them.'

'No! For God's sake They know nothing about it. That's why there had to be the secret marriage.'

'That's still no explanation,' she said coldly, while she folded up the marriage certificate and put it back into its cover again. 'So I'll keep this. I'll take it with me to show to your mother and father when I ask them for the whole story, the real story.'

'You bitch!' John Gifford yelled, and made a snatch for it, sliding on the slippery grass, and rolling down to fetch up at the dike where he lay still.

Freya looked down at him with contempt. He wasn't worth wasting any more time over, and certainly not when he was already married. Before she turned and ran back to the house she threw the packet down beside him. It glistened yellow in the light of the moon.

'Where's John?' the minister asked when

she reached him.

'That's what I've come to tell you,' she said breathlessly. 'He's lying beside the dike. He slipped and knocked his head.'

Then she ran on.

'Wait! Wait!' she shouted to the men rowing back to the *Hessa* for the last time that night. 'Come back and get me!'

'What is it, Freya?' Arne asked anxiously, bringing the little boat alongside her.

'I've made up my mind. You don't have to put into Lerwick with me ever again, Arne. This time I'm coming with you.'

'You mean, all the way? Back to Norway?'

'Back home,' she said. 'With you.'

*   *   *

At midnight Barbara waited with Christina and Alice for the Busta boat to come back. The moon sailed across a cloudless sky like a great golden galleon, lighting up the hills and valleys as bright as day. The Voe was a glassy mirror reflecting another golden galleon.

The moon on the Voe was a ghost moon, Barbara thought with a shiver. It didn't really exist. The men would row right through it, and then they would be ghosts too. She knew that was a very bad omen.

After half an hour Christina began to cough.

'It's become too chilly for you, Miss

Christina,' Alice protested. 'You must get back home and into bed.'

'Go with her, Alice,' Barbara said. 'I'll wait a few more minutes.'

The few minutes became another hour. The moon was losing its brilliant glow. A little night breeze had sprung up when she walked along the beach right round to the other side of the bay, and she noticed that instead of the hush and scatter of sand and pebbles there was silence.

The noise of the sea changed as she walked. First, there was one little surge of the waves. Then another, and another and another as the tide turned. Barbara breathed a sigh of relief. The flowing tide would help the men rowing back in this direction.

The moon was only a feathery grey disc now. Soon it would disappear altogether in the rays of the rising sun.

*　　　*　　　*

Early that Sunday morning in Busta House footsteps padded softly along the corridor. The handle of a door turned slowly and gently. After a pause the footsteps grew faster and louder as more doors were banged open carelessly and noisily. Then terrible screams began.

'My sons! My sons!' Lady Elizabeth cried. 'Thomas, where are they? It's five o'clock in

185

the morning and their beds are empty!'

Thomas Gifford did not try to pacify her. 'Betty,' he said, 'I had a bad dream. I dreamed I lost my staff, my support. It's time I was looking after my lads. Did they go to Wethersta?'

'If they did, they wouldn't have told us. There was too much talk about the white seals,' she sobbed. 'I'm frightened, Thomas!'

'I'll get James Sinclair to ride down to Wethersta and see,' he said, and went to the stables.

But James Sinclair came back with the news that although all four of their sons, John Fisken and their grieve had been at Wethersta, they had left for Busta hours ago on a flat calm sea.

*　　　*　　　*

All this time Barbara was still waiting down on the beach. In the broad daylight of another glorious morning her eyes never left the incoming waves until at last she was rewarded. The oars came drifting in. They came floating towards the shore, straight towards her. But there was something so eerie about it that her blood ran cold.

She ran to meet them with legs of lead, while black wings flapped over her head again, as they had done that first day she arrived over the sea to Busta, and again with a dreadful

186

premonition about Fisk. Then she saw the Inkster stone washed up on the beach. She was just in time to retrieve it and hide it in her shawl before Thomas Gifford arrived on the beach with his men behind him. For a minute he just stood and looked at the oars in total disbelief. Then the awful realisation came to him that it must be true . . . It must be true . . . He had lost all his remaining sons in one brutal blow of fate.

James Sinclair, standing beside him and supporting him, breathed into his ear. 'Sir, the Voe will have to be searched, and only you can organise such an immense undertaking.'

Thomas Gifford stirred out of the nightmare and rallied. There was something only he could do. 'Yes. Yes. A search. James, get every available man and fetch the dredging ships here. Busta Voe must be dredged before any more time is lost.'

*   *   *

During the uproar and the consternation of the hours that followed Barbara went up to her attic and tried to snatch some sleep, but it was hopeless. If the boat had gone down, then so had Fisk, and she thought her heart must surely break this time.

'Gone . . . Gone . . . Gone for ever,' she wept to herself, and the last one in her heart and her thoughts was John Gifford, her

187

husband.

Lady Elizabeth screamed and wailed constantly. Her husband panted up and down between the House and the beach doing his best to reassure her, but nothing could console her. He faced up to the worst part of it all, alone. He would rather his sons' bodies were found, and buried in the consecrated ground of Olnafirth Kirkyard, than be eaten by sea creatures and their bones left to moulder on the sea-bed. They *must* be found.

All day a silent crowd had gathered on the beach. All day the dredgers criss-crossed forwards and backwards across the Voe, but there was no signal from any of them. All day Barbara had watched from her attic window, shrouded like every other window in Busta, and in the evening when the people were drifting away in twos and threes, shaking their heads, she went down to the beach again, prepared to stay all night if need be, if the bodies floated in of their own accord . . .

One by one the dredgers were giving up. The light was fading fast, and down at the edge of the sea a chilly wind was blowing. Barbara stayed at one side of the beach, alone. Thomas Gifford and his men were at the other, when there was a shout from the last of the dredgers. They had found a body. Barbara stood still, frozen in dread in case she would see her beloved Fisk's drowned face. The men clambered ashore and laid down John

Gifford's body on the nearest place on the sand, at her feet.

'He must have been stuck on a ledge under the sea,' one of the men told her. 'His arm must have been upraised. We only got him because his thumb was caught in the nets.'

'Please,' she said, 'tell Mr Gifford and fetch him here.'

As soon as their backs were turned she bent over the body. His sodden jacket was still fastened. It was very hard to prise open the buttons and a gruesome task to put her hand inside it and grope for the oilskin envelope she had made herself. For a brief second, while she drew it out and secreted it, ice-cold, in her bodice, she wondered what instinct had made her make it in the first place. Then she stood back as if on guard and waited until Thomas Gifford and his party arrived.

When he looked down at the poor wreck of a man, his son and heir, it seemed to Barbara that he aged ten years in the space of one minute. He was unable to speak. James Sinclair was once again a tower of strength, propping up Mr Gifford himself and organising the others to carry John's body up to Busta House.

Barbara followed the terrible procession and went on quietly up to her attic. The first thing she did was to open the yellow envelope. Her marriage certificate was there, after all, dry and intact, the proof of her coming child's legitimacy. The next thing was to sew it into the hem of her dress to keep it safe, before she fell into her bed, exhausted.

The following morning, when the dredging continued at first light, she dressed and went out; not to the beach this time, for she knew now that there was no more hope of seeing Fisk alive, but to the Inksters' cottage. Hance himself came to the door, and she handed him the stone, wordlessly. He took it from her hand just as silently and hung it back on the nail, and when their eyes met it was in complete understanding. There had been no need for words.

Then Hilda came out. 'I'll walk you back to Busta,' she said.

'You're not coming in to—work yourself, Hilda?'

'I'll never set foot in that house again. Thank God I'll never have to, Barbara. Hanci Erasmuson and I are to be married. We're going to Canada next month.'

'Oh, Hilda! Are you happy?'

'Very happy about that,' she said with tears in her eyes, 'but Kitty should have been my bridesmaid.'

'I'm so sorry, Hilda.' Barbara put her arm around her.

'The wedding is to be very quiet, because of Kitty . . . Oh, Barbara, I know the one who did it! The others shouldn't have died! It was John Gifford. Kitty hated him. Almost the last thing she ever told me was that soon, everyone would know how bad he was.'

'Yes, and now we know what she meant,' Barbara said bitterly as they reached one of the huge iron gates in Busta's garden walls, 'but try not to brood on it. Think of Hanci instead.'

'Isn't it wonderful?' Hilda smiled, with just a hint of her usual giggle in her voice. 'And Father is pleased. I tease him and say that's because he and Hanci have the same name.'

'Yes, it's wonderful, Hilda. I hope you'll be happy in Canada.'

*   *   *

All day, as Barbara tried to carry on with her work, she kept recalling the speculations of the people who had waited on the beach before they drifted away, murmuring between themselves.

'How could it have happened, on a sea like glass?'

'Mermaids. They lure men off boats.'

'It could have been a giant skate. They've been known to flap up on board and capsize a fishing boat before today.'

'Maybe the Giffords were standing up and fighting.'

'Fighting drunk, more like.'

'Don't forget they were stopped in the Voe once before. They said themselves it was by the white seals.'

'I've never seen a white seal. Have you?'

'No. But I believe that under the sea there's another world. A world of mystery.'

*   *   *

They had been in the middle of the Voe, rowing in savage silence, when the quarrel began. Robbie started it, glaring at John. 'Let me see that yellow packet again,' he said furiously. 'I don't trust you with it.'

'What?' William cried. 'Where is it, you bastard? Have you thrown it over the side? Have we made all this effort for nothing?'

'I'll soon see,' Hay said, dropping his oar and making for his brother with his hands outstretched to search him. 'Where is it?'

John Gifford stood to his height in the boat, waving his oar above his head. 'Leave me alone!' he shouted. 'I'm sick of this. I'm sick of the lot of you, and I'm more than sick of the bloody marriage certificate. It's here in my pocket, if you must know!'

But Hay wasn't finished. 'Let's see it, then,' he shouted back, wrestling with John and his oar.

John Fisken spoke for the first time. 'This boat is going to founder.'

Nobody listened to his warning. Robbie and William threw caution to the winds and joined in the fray. Mysteriously the boat filled with water slowly sank, taking them all with it.

192

CHAPTER SIXTEEN

Bad news travels fast and it wasn't long before the news of the Busta tragedy reached Lerwick, 97 Commercial Street and the Misses Mary and Ellice Bruce.

'My God,' Miss Mary whispered. 'For such an awful thing!'

'They found John Gifford's body first, so the people are saying, and then the grieve's, but the other three Gifford sons and Mr Fisken, the minister, are at the bottom of the sea. *All four Gifford sons*, gone all at once, and for ever! Can you believe it?' Miss Ellice cried.

'Nobody left to carry on Thomas Gifford's name . . . But what about Alice and Barbara?' Miss Mary's voice held a note of panic. 'What will happen to our girls now?'

'Won't they be needed more than ever, Mary? Alice will continue to be Christina's maid. To judge from her letters they seem to be genuinely fond of each other.'

'That's true,' Miss Mary admitted grudgingly, 'but it was never Alice I worried about. Only Barbara.'

'Yes. Barbara's letters have always been written in a tearing hurry. Dutiful, but sketchy and very airy-fairy. What's she doing at this very moment, I wonder?'

'I wish I knew,' Miss Mary sighed and
193

dabbed at her eyes.

*   *   *

Barbara was thankful, when she drew back her curtains a little to the side that Saturday morning, that custom did not allow ladies to attend funerals. At eleven o'clock Mr Gifford and the men from the parish of Delting and many other parishes from all over Shetland buried his son and his grieve. She had never seen such a sombre scene before.

The boat carrying the two coffins laid side by side moved off first. She didn't even know that a boat could move so slowly. Behind it came the boats of the mourners, every man in them dressed in black, gliding along sadly and silently.

The procession went on and on until the whole Voe looked as if it moved black, and Barbara knew it was a sight so terrible that it would stay with her until the day she died. When she wept, her tears were as much because of this expression of compassion among Shetlanders, one for the other, as they were for the dead men themselves, and most of all for her beloved Fisk and the Gifford boys who would never come back now, dead or alive.

Mr Gifford had ordered that the curtains and shutters should remain closed over the windows until after the Sunday morning service at Olnafirth Kirk. Barbara was pulling on her gloves in the darkened hall when Christina, dressed all in black, protested.

'You do not have to go,' she cried. 'Nobody will expect you or any of us to go. And besides, it may put too great a strain on you at this time. Please, Barbara . . .'

'I must pay my last respects before God, Miss Christina, since we were not allowed to attend the funeral yesterday. And I do not think it will do my son any good if I lie in my bed and cry any more. He is living, and life must go on.'

Christina shivered. 'Your son, Barbara . . . Oh, I do hope so, for Busta's sake!'

Mr Gifford and James Sinclair were waiting for her to go across the Voe. The light outside seemed almost dazzling after more than a week in a darkened house although the weather had changed now, and a light drizzle was falling from a grey sky.

Even the heavens were crying, she thought, as she stepped sadly ashore and waited while Thomas Gifford shook hands with everyone who waited outside the kirk. Then he escorted her inside and the rest of the congregation followed to hear the word of God and the last benediction on the Busta men as preached by the new minister, the Reverend Mr Morrison.

When they got back home Mr Gifford dismissed everyone except James Sinclair. As they walked through the Willow Walk it seemed especially dark to Barbara, dark and somehow ominous. Mr Gifford must have been feeling it, too, because he stumbled as if he'd lost the place.

James put an arm around his master and propped him up. Barbara rushed to his other side. She didn't like the way his knees were buckling the last few steps into the House. Before they got him to the first landing on the stairs he was trailing his legs and his head had fallen sideways.

'Thomas! Thomas!' Lady Elizabeth cried when they carried him into the bedroom. 'What's happened to him?' she demanded.

'The poor old gentleman has been struck down, my lady,' James said, 'no doubt by grief. He must be got into bed, but he's a dead weight.'

'Dead? Dead?' she screeched, leaping out of the bed. 'Don't you dare utter such a word about my husband! He's not dead!' Barbara, who was trying to give James a lift, was suddenly knocked sideways by a tremendous punch on her back. 'How dare you touch him, Barbara Pitcairn!' Lady Elizabeth yelled.

'It's all right, Barbara,' said a quiet voice from the doorway. 'She doesn't know what she's saying as the result of shock upon shock. Alice and I heard all the commotion from downstairs. We'll take over here . . . Get back into bed at once, Mother, and stop that foolish shouting! Father isn't able to speak at present,

196

but he may still be able to hear, you know!'

Christina was ice-cool and calm. She and Alice helped James to get Mr Gifford into bed. Then she persuaded Lady Elizabeth to lie down beside him.

'He needs all the comfort he can get, but not another word, Mother! Do you hear? James will ride to Voe for Mr Whyte, the barber. He'll know what to do,' she said, pushing both James and Barbara out gently and closing the bedroom door firmly behind them.

'Will Mr Whyte be able to help him, James?' Barbara whispered on the way downstairs.

'Well . . . He's a great believer in leeches and bloodletting, is Mr Whyte, and he's helped me many a time when a mare's had a difficult foal.' Barbara wasn't convinced. She thought Mr Gifford would need a lot more help than that. 'But no, lassie—Mr Gifford's in God's hands now,' James added, 'if only that wife of his gives him peace to get better.'

Every day after that Barbara ran up and down the stairs to the bedroom, helping Ruby to carry peats and water for Miss Christina and Alice who were doing all the heavy nursing. They reported that his mouth was coming back to normal. It didn't droop so much to the right side, but he still couldn't speak and he had no use at all of his right arm, hand or leg.

'I'm getting worried about you, Barbara,'

Christina said a few days later. 'You shouldn't be running up and down like this, or carrying weights. It's time my parents got in more servants to help.'

'Ruby's daughter, Beenie, is ready, willing and able to come,' Barbara said.

'I'll see about it. Also, it's time they knew about your marriage to John. If they knew another little Gifford is waiting to be born it could be the very thing to cheer them both up out of all this misery. Will you bring your marriage certificate to the Long Room this evening, about eight? I'll persuade my mother to come down for an hour.'

*   *   *

'What's that girl doing here?' Lady Elizabeth scowled when Barbara entered the Long Room nervously at eight o'clock and handed her certificate over to Christina. 'And what's that she's given you?'

'Something very important, Mother, for the whole Gifford family,' Christina said, opening the document out and holding it firmly by its corners with both her hands. 'No, you may not snatch it out of my hands! It belongs to Barbara, but I'll hold it up in front of your eyes so that you can read it.'

As Lady Elizabeth read it her face went a ghastly shade of puce. She read it again, as if she didn't believe what she had seen the first time. 'What rubbish is this?' she sneered. 'Take it away! As if my John would ever have married a mere serving girl! She's just made this up! Oh, she's a cunning one, that! It's a trick.'

'No, it's not rubbish,' Christina said coldly, 'and it's not a trick. I was present at the wedding myself, as well as the boys, and you had better not call me a liar. It took place as you see on the eighth day of December last year at Symbister, and John Fisken performed the ceremony. I believe our John did mention her to you, but you refused to listen.'

'Indeed I did.'

'So he had to do it secretly, because he had already got Barbara pregnant. She expects that his child will be born in November. If it's a boy, he will be the Giffords' heir.'

'I don't care what you say, Christina. Even if it a boy, I will never accept Barbara Pitcairn as my daughter-in-law,' Lady Elizabeth vowed, and rushed back upstairs in a terrible rage.

'Pay no attention, Barbara,' Christina said. 'Sooner or later she will have to accept it, and as soon as Father is fit to understand, he will see to it that it is with open arms.'

*   *   *

Before the long, sleepless night was over Lady Elizabeth managed to calm her temper and somehow to subdue her outrage, realising that she must accept the unacceptable and believe the unbelievable, that her John—the pride of all her flock—had played her such a dirty trick, and with that detestable Barbara Pitcairn too.

But she had seen the marriage certificate, no less, with her own eyes. Oh, the impertinence of it! The duplicity of it! She lay like a ramrod beside her sleeping husband, digging her nails into the palms of her hands to stop her screaming out loud, and forced herself to lay out all the facts of what her life and come to now, and surely, never had there been a woman, a wife and a mother more cruelly treated by fate.

Here she was, lying beside a husband half dead already. All her beautiful sons were dead and gone. John had married Barbara Pitcairn behind her back. It was his child in that girl's womb. If a boy, he would be the heir to Busta. *Somehow, she must get that boy out of his mother's clutches.* But how?

*　　　*　　　*

Towards morning she dozed off for an hour or two. She slept on it. A plot was already hatched in her mind on Monday morning when she got up and smiled at her husband. Dear Thomas, who had always given her everything she had ever wanted . . . He would do this one last thing for her, too.

She went downstairs and ordered all the
200

windows to be opened to allow the fresh air in through Busta House. It seemed to everyone that this new week heralded a new beginning. Only Christina looked at her mother very suspiciously and wondered what was coming next.

Barbara tried to keep as much as possible to some routine of light housework, knitting times and walking times, and the work going on outside brought back a sense of reality and the rhythm of life.

That summer in Shetland had been two months of paradise, the meadows thick with wild flowers, the roadsides bright with pink and white clover, and the fields of grain dotted with tall ox-eye daises. The fine weather had dried up the peats on the peat-banks in the hills where the women had raised the rectangles of turf and set them into little pyramids so that the wind could blow through them.

At the end of August the men were returning from the *haaf*, the fishing-stations as near the distant fishing-grounds as possible, where they had been since May. There was plenty for them to do on the crofts of the estate when they came back. Barbara looked forward to her daily walks as August merged into September, the crucial time of the *hairst*. The oats and barley were ripe, and the men were racing to cut them before the rain came to flatten them and the wind to twist them.

She saw how shaggy the sheep on the hill were looking, now that the wool on their backs was loosening, ready to be pulled off. One day when men were shouting and dogs were barking, long lines of bleating sheep merged into streams of white flecked with brown and grey as they were driven to the pens where the *rooing*, the pulling, was done.

But at last the strings of ponies had carried home the peats in baskets slung on either side, and the stacks were built at the side of every house beside the *dess* of hay for the animals. All the work was done, the *haaf*-boats hauled up for the winter in the *noosts*, their shelters in the rocks. And Barbara, having written to her two aunts in Lerwick to tell them that she was now Mistress Gifford, the widow of John Gifford, and soon to be the mother of his child, was beginning to recover from her state of shock, in time to feel flutters in her stomach. Her baby would soon arrive.

She no longer felt frightened at the prospect, thanks, strangely, to Lady Elizabeth who had recently changed her whole attitude towards her, and was taking a great interest in her forthcoming confinement.

'I have engaged the services of Mistress Mowat for you when your time comes,' she told Barbara. 'She is the best midwife in the district. In fact, she's the only midwife hereabouts.'

'That's very kind of you, my lady.'

'Now, what would you like me to knit next? A shawl, perhaps?'

'My Aunt Ellice has promised me one of her fine shawls for the christening, my lady. A shawl is so much work—'

'Nonsense! The child will need everyday shawls as well, you know,' Lady Elizabeth said, searching in her sack of wool for a hank of a suitable colour.

It surprised Barbara that she was such a beautiful knitter, considering that she neither knitted nor sewed as a rule. In fact, she had done very little of anything except amuse herself and issue orders for other people to wait upon her hand and foot ever since she knew her.

'And what shall you name the boy when he comes?'

'I haven't decided yet. Besides, it might be a girl, my lady.'

Indeed it might, Lady Elizabeth thought, in which case there would be a short, sharp change of plans.

*   *   *

Two days before the expected date of birth Lady Elizabeth ordered Ruby and her daughter Beenie, whose ambition to work at Busta House alongside her mother had at last been fulfilled, to clear out the attic and scrub it from top to bottom. Nothing must be returned to it except the bed, and clean linen must be at hand. But when they had finished they went to tell Barbara, who had been ordered to sleep downstairs until her time came.

'I don't know what it is, dearie,' Ruby whispered anxiously, 'but she doesn't want a single nook or cranny left uncovered. Come on up quietly and have a look.'

It was true, and Barbara knew she couldn't trust the hem of her dress for a hiding place any longer, either. She must find somewhere else to put her precious marriage certificate. But where?

'Keep watch for me outside this door, Ruby,' she said. 'I won't be a minute.'

She thanked God she always wore her knitting belt around her waist, although it was now fastened at the last hole, from which dangled a tiny pair of scissors and a small pincushion. Working as fast as she could she slit the pillow's hem, pushed the yellow oilskin package deep into the heart of the feathers inside, took a needle and thread out of the pincushion and quickly sewed it up again with the tiny stitches she was famous for. It was the best she could do, she thought, when she opened the door again.

'Will you do me another big favour, Ruby?'

'Anything.'

'I can't bend down, or else I would pick up those feathers myself.'

'Mercy me! How did they get on that floor?'

204

Ruby cried in horror. 'Beenie and I left it spotless.'

'I suppose they escaped and just floated out of the pillow, Ruby. Don't worry. Sometimes they do.'

On the afternoon of the third day of November Barbara went into labour. Lady Elizabeth herself helped her up to her attic, and received her clothes as she removed them. Then, clad in a white pinafore herself, she handed her a clean nightgown, and Barbara lay down.

'Mistress Mowat hasn't come yet,' Lady Elizabeth said, 'but I'll help you until she arrives. I suppose I know even more than she does, in any case, after having fourteen children of my own.'

The night wore on, the pains got worse and worse until they got so bad that Barbara wouldn't have known whether Mistress Mowat was there or not. She was just so grateful that Lady Elizabeth was as good a midwife as she was a knitter.

Lady Elizabeth smiled down at her, judging that the baby's head would appear in less than half an hour, and in the meantime she had worked out where that marriage certificate must be—where it had to be, for there was nowhere else.

And now Barbara was too far gone to know what was happening. She removed the pillow from under Barbara's head and examined it minutely. Yes, there were the differently coloured stitches in the hem, just as she had surmised. She slit the pillow open, put in her hand and groped about until her fingers found the oilskin envelope which she hid in the bodice of her dress. Then she quickly sewed it up again, with tiny stitches which could easily rival Barbara's.

'The head's coming,' she told her at eight o'clock in the morning. 'Now, push. Yes, that's right! Push again! Again!' A few minutes later she cut the cord, wrapped the baby in a cloth and held it up to let the mother see. 'It's a boy!' she said. 'Isn't it wonderful? It's a beautiful little boy!'

The only disadvantage was, Barbara Pitcairn would have to stay on, now. The boy would need a nurse, and what better nurse than his own mother? Until the time came when she would become dispensable.

'It's a boy,' she opened the attic door to tell Ruby and the other maids gathered outside. 'My grandson is born, the heir to Busta!'

'And Miss Barbara?' Ruby asked. 'How is she?'

'Well enough—now, nobody comes in here until Mistress Mowat arrives. Of course, she is too late for the birth. I delivered the baby myself. In half an hour we will have some breakfast sent up here. I'll wait with the mother and child.'

Very anxious about the well-being of the

baby, all day long she showed Barbara how to breast-feed him, how to get up his wind, how to put on his little napkins, how to change them, and how to bathe him, all the while supporting his head.

And still Mistress Mowat hadn't come.

'Very strange,' Lady Elizabeth said, and camped out in what used to be Alice's attic next door, not allowing anyone else in for fear they gave the baby a cold. 'And now it's snowing hard,' she told Barbara. 'Mistress Mowat won't be able to get here until it thaws . . . What's the matter?'

'I feel sick.' Barbara said, gazing at all the feathers gathering in a little heap in the corner, and dreading the reason why.

'You're not sick at all. Control yourself, for the sake of the child. By the way, have you decided upon a name for him?'

'His name is Gideon. I've always liked that name.'

'It is usual to name a boy for his own father. According to you yourself, that should be John.'

'His name is Gideon,' Barbara repeated, and lay back on her pillow feeling exhausted and very ill.

'Have it your own way,' Lady Elizabeth snapped.

She left the attic for the first time for a week to go downstairs and send for James Sinclair. 'Now that the snow is going, ride over to

Mistress Mowat and ask her why she didn't attend the birth,' she ordered.

'Why I didn't attend the birth?' Mistress Mowat exclaimed in sheer amazement, putting on her shawl and preparing to ride back with him. 'I was never asked. This is the first I've heard of it.'

'You'd better not say that in Her Majesty's hearing,' James said grimly. 'That's her story, for some reason, and she's sticking to it.'

When she was sure that she was alone at last with her baby, Barbara rose out of her bed and examined her pillow. The stitches were different again.

She ripped it open, but her marriage certificate had gone.

CHAPTER SEVENTEEN

Mistress Mowat cast an expert eye over mother and child. The baby seemed to be perfectly normal and his colour was good, but the young mother was a different story, lying there pale and listless and, if she was not mistaken, with a face blotched with tears. Of course it was only to be expected when the child's father, rumoured to be John Gifford, was dead and gone. Poor peerie lass, and her so young and bonnie!

'Ah, for such a pretty baby!' she said. 'And

how are you feeling yourself, lass?'

'Sick most of the time, Mistress Mowat.'

'You shouldn't be. Lady Busta delivered your baby, I understand?'

'Yes.'

'Did she get everything away after the birth?'

'Everything?'

'The skin the baby was lying in inside your womb. The afterbirth—did it come away?'

'I don't know about that, Mistress Mowat. Lady Elizabeth is the only one who would know. All I do know is that I feel hollow inside, now that Gideon's born, and I've been bleeding ever since.'

'That sounds about right, then,' the midwife said doubtfully. 'Well, I can see that my job here is to get you well and back on your feet again. Are you eating?'

'Not much,' Barbara smiled wanly.

'Think about this peerie fellow here! If you don't eat, then you can't feed him. He still depends on you entirely, Miss Barbara.'

*   *   *

It was well through November, and Gideon was almost a month old and thriving before Mistress Mowat departed. Barbara still felt shaky, and defeated. She wasn't herself at all. Alice and Miss Christina had been to admire Gideon when he was newly born, but now they were making themselves very scarce. She longed to tell her troubles to someone she could trust. She missed Fisk more than ever. *He* would have listened to her. *He* would have made her feel better, right away.

Then one day, with Gideon in her arms, she met Alice creeping dolefully along to Miss Christina's sitting room.

'Alice,' she said, 'my marriage certificate has gone. It's disappeared. I think Miss Christina should know that I believe Lady Elizabeth stole it.'

'Oh, no,' Alice shuddered. 'Please don't give Miss Christina any more problems. She's upset enough as it is.'

'Why? What's happened?'

'John Bruce Stewart has written to say that his wife died at the time of the drownings. He didn't tell her when it happened because she was in deep mourning for her brothers, and then Mr Gifford fell ill on the top of it.'

'But that was six months ago, Alice! The mourning is over now for both of them. They can get married at last.'

'So John Bruce Stewart says, but he doesn't know Miss Christina like I do,' Alice said sadly. 'She won't leave Busta until her father is better, and besides, her mother wouldn't let her go until that happy day.'

'But he's greatly improved already! You both know that! And what about you, Alice?'

'Me?' Alice tickled Gideon's chin and then

210

bent down to kiss it. 'I'm not important, Barbara. I've always hated it here at Busta. Many a time I would have thrown myself into the Voe if it hadn't been for Christina.'

'What?' Barbara cried, appalled.

'It's true. My fate depends on hers. If she goes to Whalsay, then so do I. She won't tackle her mother about your certificate. She won't rock the boat, I can tell you. All she wants is to get out of here in peace and pleasure, and all I want is to go with her.'

*   *   *

It was the following January when Gideon was nearly three months old and Mr Gifford was partially recovered that Lady Elizabeth deemed the time was right to tell him he was a grandfather. John had got Barbara Pitcairn into trouble, she said, but at least she had produced a son as the result.

From that minute on events moved rapidly.

He was a grandfather! When Thomas Gifford saw Gideon for the first time he wept for joy. 'Oh, for such a fine peerie man!' he said, over and over again, and after that refused all help. He insisted on walking by himself with the aid of his stick. Now, he had something to live for again.

Christina Gifford finally gave herself a shake out of her doldrums and sent word that she would accept John Bruce Stewart as her

211

husband most joyfully. Even Alice was smiling again.

'Oh, Miss Christina,' Barbara said, hugging her when the day of departure came, 'I hope you will be very happy. I know you will. I'm so happy for you!'

'Thank you, dear, but I've had terrible pangs in my heart about taking Alice with me, separating her from you, her sister.'

'She is happy with you, Miss Christina. She wants to go,' Barbara said, and stood waving to them both when they sailed off to their new life in Whalsay.

But when she turned back from the pier and made her way up to Busta House she had never felt so alone and lonely in all her life. She couldn't have burdened Christina with her immense disaster. She wouldn't have spoiled her joy. But her health deteriorated even more with the worry that Gideon could now be construed as illegitimate when she had nothing to prove that he wasn't.

*   *   *

After so many twists of fortune Barbara's life took another downturn the Sunday after Christina and Alice went away. Mr Gifford, still unable to clamber aboard the boat, didn't offer to go to the kirk across the Voe at Olnafirth. He elected to stay at home and watch Gideon who was in Beenie's charge.

212

For once, Lady Elizabeth joined Barbara on the pier, and they made the journey in silence. When they stepped out of the boat the new minister, the Reverend Mr Morrison, was waiting. Although she hadn't seen him there, Barbara had been told by Ruby that he had been at Busta already, and had spent a long time closeted with Lady Elizabeth. Now, she took an instant dislike to the stout, pompous little man rubbing his hands together while he spoke in an oily voice.

'My dear Lady Busta, what an honour!' he said, taking her arm and leading her into the kirk. Barbara followed behind, ignored. 'Of course, you have your own pew, the Busta pew—but today, perhaps you would like to sit here where you would get the best view?'

The best view of what, Barbara wondered? She was following Lady Elizabeth into a pew in the middle of the kirk when Mr Morrison suddenly gripped her by one arm and signalled to an elder to take her by the other.

The congregation hissed in disbelief and Barbara was struck dumb with horror to find herself up on the stool in the Penitents' Box with the door locked behind her, looking straight into Lady Elizabeth's cold, triumphant black eyes.

She gripped the wooden rail in front of her until her knuckles stood out white, but she felt nothing. Lady Elizabeth's eyes faded into nothingness while Barbara floated in some sort

213

of shocked limbo. She heard nothing. She saw nothing, until her eyes focused on the minister's mouth opening and closing like a goldfish in a bowl. She could see that his face was turning a mottled red. She watched his finger of scorn pointing at her and it meant nothing until, as if a door had suddenly opened to let the sound come out, her sense of hearing came back with a rush.

'An abomination! A whore!' Mr Morrison was shouting.

She wanted to protest her innocence and Gideon's innocence and to shout back that she was a married woman, that she had been John Gifford's wife, but at that moment the dark eyes of Lady Elizabeth, full of hatred, swam back into focus and Barbara knew the battle was lost. That woman had stolen the only proof there was.

As Mr Morrison's voice soared to the rafters continuing his vicious tirade Hance Inkster stood up. So did his wife, Gracie. Then they walked out. It was unheard of, unthinkable, but they led a silent protest. The whole congregation followed them and Mr Morrison was left yelling and shouting only to Lady Elizabeth and the elders, and to Barbara who had her hands over her ears while the tears poured down her face.

He stopped at last, and in the deafening silence that followed the shame-faced elders unlocked the door and helped Barbara out

214

into the waiting arms of Mistress Gracie Inkster. Barbara stood with her head on Gracie's shoulder, almost fainting, while Mr Morrison escorted Lady Elizabeth past a congregation fast turning into a snarling mob.

'Barbara, we'll take you back in our boat,' Hance said, hurrying her away. 'You're not going with that awful snake of a Gifford woman. She was never very high in anyone's estimation, but after this day's work she's at rock bottom.'

They took her back to Busta and put her into Ruby's arms, with a brief description of what had happened. 'Look after her and her baby, Ruby,' Mistress Gracie said tearfully as they left.

'Ho! Don't you worry,' Ruby assured them. 'I have my own little methods. I'll make the old bitch pay!'

*   *   *

Already, Lady Elizabeth knew she had made a huge blunder. It had all gone wrong. It had all backfired on her, and in the weeks and months that followed she could tell by Ruby's contemptuous eyes that it had better be a long, long time before she tried anything else to hurt Barbara. As it was, she was lucky that no one dared to tell her husband about it. It might have killed him, and she needed him, to carry out the plan from which she had never deviated all along.

No amount of gentle persuasion and encouragement from all her friends could warm Barbara's heart after such a humiliation, and she retreated into a little world of her own with Gideon. And, like a lucky charm, Gideon smiled his way into everyone's affection. The general opinion was the same as Ruby's Beenie's.

'He's just a peerie darling.'

'There are plenty of toys somewhere in this house,' Mr Gifford told Barbara. 'As our children grew up I could never bear to throw them away. It would have been like throwing away their childhoods,' he confided, wiping away the tears that came so easily since his illness, 'and God knows their childhoods were snuffed out soon enough . . . Take my keys and ask Ruby. She'll know.'

At one year old Gideon loved the soft, cuddly toys, the knitted stuffed teddy bears and rabbits, but his favourite was a little doll, dressed like a Shetland 'wifie' as he called it. When he was two, he took to the bats and balls, but the best thing in his life so far was the old rocking horse. He spent hours on its back in the Long Room, and Barbara was looking after him there one morning when Ruby flounced in.

'Would you look at the mess I'm in?' she demanded. 'Look at my pinny! It's covered with bits and strings of that sacking.'

'What sacking, Ruby?'

'Oh, nothing else would do but we had to pack up that old writing desk in the Giffords' bedroom and cover it with canvas to go over the sea. Beenie and I have been hours at it. It's going to Miss Christina—I beg her pardon—*Lady Symbister*, as Her Majesty calls her!'

'I wonder why?' Barbara said. 'Christina has beautiful furniture of her own, now.'

'Well, there's the men carrying it down to the boat,' Ruby said, pointing out of the window. 'It'll be in Whalsay by nightfall, and I shouldn't think Miss Christina will thank her for it, either.'

From an upstairs window Lady Elizabeth was also watching the men heaving the desk onto the boat. It might be old, she thought, and a bit worm-eaten, but it was the only one in the house with a secret drawer. That was where she had hidden that wretched marriage certificate, and she had put a letter of instruction for Christina in the top drawer. Thank God to have got it all out of Busta House and shipped off safely to Whalsay. Thank God Thomas had never seen it or known anything about it.

Whatever Ruby knew or suspected she wouldn't dare open her mouth. Her job, not to mention her daughter Beenie's job, depended upon it. And even if Ruby had gossiped about it to the other maidservants, they would keep their mouths shut too, for the same reason.

She breathed a huge sigh of relief. The whole sorry business was almost out of her hands. *Only two more parts of her plan still to be carried out* . . . But she had learned her lesson; to tread carefully, let events dictate the pace and to have patience. Sooner or later it would all be successfully accomplished.

*　　*　　*

'Why on earth would my mother send me this nasty old writing desk?' Christina asked Alice. 'I never liked it.'

'But then, she's never been to Symbister House to see that you have two beautiful desks of your own. By the way, look at the legs!'

'Worms!' Christina gazed at it in horror. 'Well, it can't go into any room in this house. It can't even go into the attic. The worms would eat their way through the very floor!'

'So what shall we do with it?'

'Tell the servants to wrap it up again and put it out into the shed along with all the other unwanted furniture.'

'You're not even going to look in the drawers?'

'Hm!' Christina said. 'This is all wasting time, Alice, when the seamstress is on her way for the last fitting of your wedding gown. But yes,' pulling open the top drawer, 'there is something here, a packet. Listen to this!

For Christina Bruce Stewart,
Lady Symbister,
To be opened by her after my death.
Elizabeth Gifford,
Lady of Busta.

Really, Alice, isn't that just like my mother? Dramatic as ever! Anyway she isn't dead yet. That event may be a long way off, but your marriage to the best skipper in Whalsay is not, and there's a lot to be seen to. What would Lowrie Irvine think if you weren't ready next Sunday?'

'Oh, I'll be ready! I'll marry him in my petticoat if I have to!' Alice smiled radiantly.

All the same, while she was being fitted for her wedding gown, anxious little thoughts kept darting in and out of Alice's mind. Barbara had been so convinced that Lady Elizabeth had stolen her marriage certificate . . . Miss Christina had known nothing about that, of course, but could it be hidden in that rotten old desk, by any chance?

What a far-fetched suspicion! And anyway, how could she be thinking such dark thoughts at such a happy time in her life? Alice dismissed them.

No doubt the certificate had turned up at Busta long ago.

CHAPTER EIGHTEEN

Gideon was three and a half years old and Barbara was taking him for a walk one lovely sunny day when they met Mr Gifford and James Sinclair leading the little Shetland pony out of the stables for his daily run around the park.

'Hakki's getting old now,' Mr Gifford said, 'but he's always loved children, and always been very gentle with them.'

Barbara smiled and nodded. She didn't like to remind the old gentleman that Hay had taught her to ride on Hakki and of all the fun they'd had.

'I know a peerie man who would love to get up on his back if his mother would allow it,' Mr Gifford went on.

'It looks as though I have very little say in the matter,' Barbara smiled when James put an ecstatic Gideon on a real horse. 'How can I refuse?'

'Well then, bairns—enjoy yourselves! James, look after them both,' Mr Gifford said after a while, hobbling off with the aid of his stick.

'Hakki's delighted and Gideon's delighted,' James observed as the little pony trotted along gently and Barbara walked along beside them breathing in the scents of the summer flowers. 'And now it's time to take Master Gideon inside, Miss Barbara,' James said suddenly. 'We have an unwelcome visitor.'

But it was too late. A man was riding towards them.

'Who is it?' Barbara asked, pulling Gideon down off Hakki's back.

'Andrew Gifford of Ollaberry. Mr Gifford's brother. Lady Elizabeth hasn't allowed him inside Busta for years. He only upsets the master,' James was muttering when the man rode up and dismounted.

'And who's this?' he asked rudely, gazing at Barbara out of bloodshot eyes.

'Not that it's any of your business, sir, but it is Barbara Pitcairn, the mother of Gideon here, and I think it would be better if you left now.'

'Don't worry, I'm going. But I think the lady of the house wants to speak to me first.'

Lady Elizabeth was marching across the lawns with a turn of speed which surprised everyone. 'Take the child inside,' she snapped at Barbara. 'And James, put the pony back in the stables. I'll deal with this man. Why are you here?' she demanded, turning to her brother-in-law.

'To inquire about my brother's health, of course. Why else?'

'You don't give a damn about him,' she said. 'You would be happy if he was dead.'

'That's right,' he said, giving back as good as he was getting, 'I would! When he finally dies

221

I'll be the Laird of Busta, madam! Don't forget that!'

'Not now. We have a grandson now, as you saw.'

'I saw he was the picture of John Gifford. But then, John Gifford was never married, was he? That child is illegitimate. He cannot inherit. I am the next of kin.'

James and young Eddie Leask rushed up at that moment brandishing their whips. 'Get out!' James said, with his arm raised.

'I'm going, I'm going,' Ollaberry laughed and mounted his horse again. 'I only came to tell her Ladyship the news.' He fixed Lady Elizabeth with his drunken eyes. 'My son Patrick and your daughter Andrina were married yesterday, madam—and not before time. The little minx is pregnant. What do you think of *that*? Even if I am never the Laird of Busta myself, Patrick will be!'

With that, he cantered off, laughing. Lady Elizabeth certainly wasn't laughing. It was the most dangerous position the Giffords of Busta had ever been in. Every word Andrew of Ollaberry had said was true.

But she held a trump card.

It was time to put the next part of her plan into action. So far, except for a few mistakes and hiccups, everything had gone swimmingly. But there was always the element of surprise, something she hadn't allowed for in the unknown future.

222

Well, there was only one way to find out about the unknown future that she knew about. Like it or not, she would have to consult the fortune-teller. Not that she believed in such superstitious nonsense—at least, not entirely—but like every other Shetlander, she almost did. So she would send for Minna. Of course, the consultation would be held in the kitchen, well out of Thomas's sight and earshot.

'You may go early this evening,' she dismissed the maids imperiously when Minna arrived, and made tea with the very tea-leaves she considered the servants stole from her hoard every day of the week.

Merren and Ruby hid in the barn next to the kitchen with the door open so that they could hear Minna reading Lady Elizabeth's cup.

'The leaves tell the past and the present as well as the future, you know,' the old fortune-teller began with a frown.

'Get on with it, woman! I know about the past and the present. It's the future that concerns *me*.'

'Ah! But very often it's your past that influences your future, my lady, and what I see here,' Minna squinted at the cup, 'is something in your recent past that will influence the House of Busta with bad luck for generations to come. It looks like a paper in a box. I would show it to you just disappearing over the rim of your cup, but it's unlucky.'

223

'A box? A box? I know nothing of a box!'

'I think you do, my lady. It was a very big box, and you sent it over water to someone close to you. The paper was hidden inside it.'

'Rubbish!' Lady Elizabeth's face went pale.

'The tragedy is,' Minna went on inexorably, 'it won't be found by the one you sent it to. That's part of the bad luck. In fact, it won't be found for many years—and then, by your bitterest enemy.'

'I have no enemy, mistress.'

'No? I see the initials A G and O beside the box. Andrew Gifford of Ollaberry, perhaps?'

'Ho! Is that all?' Lady Elizabeth heaved a deep sigh of relief. 'I saw Ollaberry off long ago!' By this time she was sweating although she still didn't believe the old woman's warning. 'But you spoke of many years of bad luck. None of our generation have many years before us either for good luck or bad.'

'But our grandchildren have.'

'Are you talking about Gideon?'

'Miss Barbara's Gideon, yes. Gideon Pitcairn.'

'*Gideon Gifford*—or he soon will be, I assure you. And that's what I want to know: will he live on here as the Laird of Busta?' Lady Elizabeth asked, clenching her trembling hands.

'I see children at the feet of a tall, happy young man here at Busta. But all his life he will be plagued with worry over this never-ending feud. I hope you have found your fortune to your liking, my lady?' Minna asked, holding out her hand.

'The good bits, yes. The bad bits, no. So I won't be crossing your palm with silver, my good woman. However, you may have another cup of tea before you go,' Lady Elizabeth said as she swept out.

*   *   *

'Stupid, stupid bitch,' Ruby muttered in the barn. 'Can't she see that if Ollaberry gets his hands on that marriage certificate to prove Gideon legitimate, he will destroy it and set himself up as the true heir?'

'Oh God,' Merren whispered, 'I can see it all coming. I believe every word Minna said. Well, come on, Ruby! Her Ladyship's gone now. Let's go back inside.'

They found Minna still sitting in the kitchen, her face drained.

'We heard it all, Minna.'

'It wasn't just the tea-leaves, lasses. I had a vision of the future. Her Ladyship's evil and cunning will reach out for generations to come. It will be a case of the biter bitten in the end. Then she'll be turning in her grave, believe me.'

'Have another cup of tea,' Merren said briskly, trying to repress a shudder, 'and then we'll walk you home.'

Not a natural-born diplomat by any means, nevertheless Lady Elizabeth used every ounce of finesse she possessed to acquaint her husband of the desperate situation, and of the fact that the grooms had seen off his brother, Andrew of Ollaberry, with whips.

Then she added her deadly postscript.

'Our Andrina is expecting a child next, Thomas, and since she went and got married to that Patrick Gifford—against our wishes— the baby will be legitimate.'

'Well, that's something, I suppose,' he sighed, demonstrating to his wife that he still wasn't well enough to grasp all the implications of what she'd tried to tell him in a roundabout way. 'It means that I will be one grandfather to her baby, and my wretched brother the other.'

'Yes,' she added as gently as she could, giving him time to allow it to sink in. 'It also means that if Andrina has a boy, he will be our heir, or so Andrew of Ollaberry has just been bragging.'

'What nonsense! Gideon will be the heir to Busta! Neither my brother nor any of his issue will inherit.'

'Dearest Thomas, you are much too clever to allow such a thing to happen. As you say, Gideon should inherit our estate and our fortune.'

'But how can he, when he's a bastard?' he asked in despair.

At the very thought, Mr Gifford became quite agitated. Lady Elizabeth knew that in two seconds she could have told him the truth, that John had entered into a secret marriage with Barbara Pitcairn, and that Gideon was his perfectly legitimate grandchild. But she had other fish to fry and was not to be deterred, even for his sake.

'You can overcome even that obstacle, dearest husband.'

'How?'

'We could adopt Gideon as our own.'

'Oh, my God, Betty!' he said, dissolving into tears. 'My God . . . What would I do without you? Of course, we could adopt him. But what about Barbara?'

'You would be doing her a huge favour, as well. How could she give Gideon the lifestyle you can give him here in Busta?'

She would have to give him time to digest this conversation, she could see that. He would have to be gently coaxed further into believing that he had thought of the whole thing himself. She calculated that would take another week. Another week of endless discussions . . .

At the end of it he was more like his old self again.

'My dear Betty,' he said, 'there is a solution to all of this. There is always a solution to

227

every problem and usually the most straightforward one is best. We need an heir of our own and Gideon is of our own blood. His mother will never be able to provide for him. Therefore, we shall set the legalities in motion to simply adopt him.'

'You know best, dearest Thomas.'

And that was the next step of her plot taken care of, she gloated.

'Fetch me paper and pen,' he added, 'and together we will draft a letter to David Balfour, our advocate in Edinburgh.'

It took six months for the adoption to come through and even when it did the Giffords decided to say nothing to Barbara, who lived on quietly in Busta House, loving her son and attending to all his needs. With that, she was satisfied, for Gideon was her whole world now.

In the summer of 1755 when Gideon was almost seven years old his great passion was for boats. His grandfather got the old toy yachts out of the cupboards for him to play with and his grandmother made new tiny sails for him to sail them. His grandparents doted on him.

Most days Barbara went down to the edge of the Voe and, if there was any wind at all, helped him to sail his boats in the rock pools left after the tides. Sometimes the sea could be kind, she thought one very hot afternoon when the toy boats were idle and the sun dried up the sea weeds. They smelled salty and full of iodine when they popped the bladder-wrack under their bare feet.

Gideon had wandered away with his little bucket when Mr Gifford came down to the shore to join them. 'What's he doing today?' he asked.

'Catching crabs, sir.'

'And how are you, my dear? My wife and I have not thought you to be looking too well, lately.'

'I'm all right, thank you, sir.'

'So,' he said, gazing out over the Voe, 'we wondered if perhaps you could do with a change? How would you like to go and visit your aunts in Lerwick?'

Barbara's heart did a somersault. To go back to Lerwick? To see her aunts again, and show them Gideon? And oh! How tired and weary she was, living at Busta under Lady Elizabeth's poisonous eyes!

'Oh, sir,' she said, 'how wonderful! I should like that very much!'

'I'll arrange it for two days from now, during this fine run of weather when the glass is so high. Mr Peter Williamson, who brought you here, will take you back. You agree?'

'With all my heart, Mr Gifford. Thank you, and Lady Elizabeth.'

'I don't trust them,' Ruby said dolorously when Barbara started to pack her bags, Gideon's first and then at the last minute her own. 'I wish you wouldn't go. The Giffords are strung up to high heaven because you're going. There's something in the wind. There's something not right about this, Barbara. Please don't go!'

'It's only for two weeks, Ruby. Then I'll be back.'

'Oh, yes?'

'I promise.'

It was another fine day when with Gideon holding her hand Barbara walked down to the pier at the appointed time. Peter Williamson and Samuel were waiting in their boat. What wind there was would be behind them. All was set fair, but to her surprise a convoy of people accompanied her. The two grooms were there, Ruby and Beenie who looked very unhappy, Mr Gifford and even Lady Elizabeth. What had she done to deserve all this attention, Barbara wondered?

'You have all your things?' Mr Gifford asked her.

'Yes, sir.'

'Then we wish you well, Barbara Pitcairn. Enjoy your time in Lerwick,' he said as Mr Williamson handed her into the boat.

'Thank you,' Barbara smiled and held out her arms for Gideon.

'There's just one thing. We didn't want to distress you by telling you at the time, but my wife and I adopted Gideon two years ago— James!'

James Sinclair snatched Gideon off the pier

and put him into Lady Elizabeth's waiting arms.

'Gideon!' Barbara screamed.

'He will not be going with you,' Lady Elizabeth said coldly. 'He is Gideon Pitcairn no longer. He is Gideon Gifford, and ours now. This is where he belongs.'

She was smiling as she carried Gideon back up to Busta in her powerful arms. He smiled back, feeling perfectly safe with his dear Mama as she had taught him to call her.

'Is Papa coming?' he asked innocently.

Mr Gifford was still talking to Mother on the boat. She didn't seem to understand that she had to go away by herself for a while. But he did. He was a big boy now. Mama told him so, and Papa told him that one day this big house would be all his. He would never leave it, like Mother was doing.

Ruby and Beenie stood transfixed. They were as horror-stricken as Barbara was. 'How could she?' Ruby began to cry. 'She's taken the bairn away from his mother—James Sinclair, do something!'

'I'm doing what I was told to do, the same as we all have to,' he said bitterly as he and young Eddie pushed the struggling Barbara back into the boat and strapped her down. 'I'm really sorry, lass,' he muttered, shame-faced.

Peter and Samuel Williamson set off immediately, the strong strokes of their oars taking her further and further away from

231

Gideon, her only reason for living. For a long time Barbara could only stare in total shock as Busta House became smaller and smaller and then disappeared from sight.

'What did they mean?' she appealed to Peter Williamson. 'Did they mean that I will never go back again? That I will never see my son again?'

He couldn't reply because of the tears that were choking him. His son Samuel was shouting and pointing excitedly.

'Father! Father! The white seals! They're here again, hundreds of them!'

'Oh, please don't struggle so, Miss Barbara,' Peter Williamson begged with a restraining hand on her thrashing body.

'Let me go! Let me go! If I can't be with my Gideon I just want to die!' Barbara screamed.

The boat rocked violently and the white seals slapped the sides of it in a perfect flurry of agitation. The more she screamed the more they leaped up out of the water and splashed back down again sending great waves of spray across the boat. Much more of it, Peter saw, and they would be swamped altogether.

But Samuel was too green and inexperienced to see the danger. 'See how angry they are!' he shouted, standing up and trying to push them away with his oar. 'Stop that!' his father snapped. 'You're only making them angrier still. Sit down and row, Samuel. Help me to get this boat safely to Lerwick, and for God's sake keep your voice down!'

'Why? They're only seals. They can't hear me,' Samuel said sullenly, pulling on his oar.

'Oh, can't they?'

Peter's face was set grim. He had seen many strange things on the sea, but none so strange as these creatures encircling them all the way. They only dived under the waves when the boat reached Lerwick harbour.

*   *   *

Miss Mary and Miss Ellice Bruce answered the knock on the door and then staggered back in consternation.

Mr Williamson stood there in tears, holding up the half-fainting form they scarcely recognised as their beautiful young niece of nine or ten years ago.

'It was a nightmare trip down from Busta,' he told them. 'Who would have believed that on a lovely day like this it was the worst trip of my life. Miss Barbara has screamed and cried herself almost senseless. She would have thrown herself overboard if she hadn't been strapped down.'

'You mean, they tied her to the boat?' Miss Mary cried, helping him to carry Barbara inside. 'Like a common criminal, just a prisoner?'

'Why, for God's sake?' Miss Ellice burst into tears. 'And where's Gideon?'

'The Giffords kept him. They say they have adopted him,' Peter Williamson wiped his eyes and blew his nose. 'They have kept the child and thrown his mother out. In all my life I never saw such cruelty in Shetland before.'

*   *   *

Gossip was rife in Lerwick for the next ten days. Barbara Pitcairn was back at 97 Commercial Street, just a crumpled wreck with no sign of a son, if there had ever been a son, whatever the Misses Bruce had boasted—they whispered, digging each other in the ribs and cackling. The Pitcairns had got their comeuppance. Barbara was no longer a lady, lording it in the likes of Busta House. She should never have been sent there in the first place.

It was a terrible ten days for the Pitcairn family, when Barbara seemed to be in some kind of coma of despair, when she wouldn't or couldn't speak to her aunts. But they still heard the gossip, and they relayed it back to her. The more she heard of it the more her old spirit came to her aid.

'Dear Aunts,' she said, 'don't pay any attention. Something else will happen for them to talk about very soon, if the world goes round as usual. But between you and me, the sorry fact is that everything they have said is quite true. The Giffords did steal my Gideon

234

away from me, and then they got rid of me.'

'And none too gently, by all accounts,' Aunt Mary said grimly. 'Is there nothing you can do to get your son back again? Is there not some law against kidnapping? For that is what this amounts to.'

'They have gone about it legally, Aunt Mary. And, as they pointed out, they can give Gideon a far better life than I ever could. I cannot deny him that, nor his inheritance. I have accepted that, now.'

'You will stay here in your own home,' Aunt Ellice said. 'We should never have let you go. We only did, for exactly the same reason: to give you and Alice a better life, for we are still as poor as church mice.'

'They cannot be so hard-hearted as to never let me see my son again,' Barbara wept, 'but it is all I can do, to live here with you, dear Aunts, hoping and praying for that happy day, and helping you all I can.'

CHAPTER NINETEEN

In the loving care of Aunt Mary and Aunt Ellice Barbara survived somehow, while the days stretched into weeks and the weeks into months. Surely, she thought, the Giffords would allow Gideon to visit her on his seventh birthday in November. But his birthday came and went without a word.

Well, they must relent at Christmas, then. Of all times of the year Christmas was the time for a Mother and Child, and the Giffords were Christians, if nothing else. And when it came, there was a ray of hope. Barbara received presents from Mr Gifford, and a letter.

He sent down a side of beef which would certainly help her impoverished aunts through the worst of the winter, a sack of raw wool which she could spin and then knit into garments to sell, and twelve bags of peats. It was kind of him.

Far more important than that was his letter. She tore it open with shaking hands. Money fell out on the floor, but the words, the all-important news of her son, blurred before her eyes.

'You must know that before the end of 1753 I executed a deed of entail, leaving the estate to my grandson, procreate of the body of John Gifford, my eldest lawful son, and a bond for £10,000 in Gideon Gifford's favour was made out over the estate of Busta, in case any legal difficulty might arise to prevent him taking possession.'

'Oh, God,' Barbara thought, 'how could I ever compete with that?'

'In return for your discretion over the whole matter, now closed, I shall send you a small annuity, as well as part of a beast and raw wool every Christmas.'

'Gideon is well and happy. I trust that you will leave him in peace.'

*   *   *

And that was all, about Gideon. No promise of a visit, either way. Barbara's hopes were so dashed that not even Mr Gifford's payment for her silence could make up for such a disappointment.

Her aunts tut-tutted over the letter and tried to calm her down. Aunt Mary took the wool and started the spinning process right away. Aunt Ellice cured the beef in brine and then hung it from the rafters to smoke in the peat-reek. Their industry and quiet acceptance of their fate put Barbara to shame, and she was glad she could give them the small pittance Mr Gifford had sent her. It was a very godsend to them.

Eventually she was able to accompany them to the tea-parties of the town. Always attentive to her dress, Barbara would occasionally go out in the finery she used to wear in Busta, which Lady Elizabeth had tossed down to Lerwick contemptuously after she forced her to leave. At home she received visitors in a fine yellow silk gown with a white-flowered laced apron, with more lace in her cap, handkerchief and ruffles.

So, for a few brave years Barbara blossomed in the Indian summer of her life, when her hair shone like a bird's wing again and some colour came back to her cheeks. She always said it was because of her twice daily solitary walks, the best times of the day for her, when she could roam along the shore and communicate with her friends, the white seals.

In reality those were the times when she dwelt upon her son, seeing him in her mind's eye from birth until he was almost seven years old, that and no further. Those were the times when she shed her pent-up tears in private, and nobody ever intruded upon her. They lost interest in her, for she never discussed her past with anyone. She was keeping to her side of the bargain.

*   *   *

By 1759 Andrew Gifford of Ollaberry had drunk himself to death. Nobody was surprised at that, but they were surprised that his son, Patrick, and Patrick's wife Andrina fast followed in his footsteps. They had three children by now, Andrew aged six, Thomas aged four and Elizabeth aged two.

The three children were found screaming in the house of Ollaberry while their parents had evidently fallen in the fire in a drunken state and burned to death.

'They are our grandchildren, too,' Lady Elizabeth sighed. 'So much is the pity.'

'I have always been seen as a charitable

man, Betty. We can do no less than take them in. God knows they haven't had much of a home at Ollaberry,' Thomas Gifford said.

But he never felt happy after that, with these three little cuckoos in the nest, and to make matters worse, no matter how pleasant Gideon was towards his three new cousins, the oldest boy especially hated him with all his might and main.

'He's jealous,' Lady Elizabeth said, and smacked Andrew hard.

'We always brought up our children kindly, Betty,' Mr Gifford objected weakly. 'We always took them with good, and never with ill.'

'I hate him,' she said venomously. 'He's Andrew Gifford of Ollaberry's grandson, isn't he? I can never forget that.'

But she had to forget that, and a lot more, when Thomas Gifford had his second stroke early in 1760, and passed away. She grieved for a husband who had been an outstanding man in Shetland, who had done so much for so many people, and who had loved her all his days. But she cut short her period of mourning. Her old king was dead. Long live the young king, in the shape of Gideon Gifford, the new Laird of Busta, aged twelve. She still had a lot of work to do, to guide him into his future life.

Andrew hated him more than ever. But it would be a long time before he was able to get out of Busta and live his own life. And tragedy struck again, when little Elizabeth, Andrew's darling sister, wandered off into the Voe and was drowned.

But Lady Busta was indomitable. She rose above it all and ruled her household with a rod of iron.

*　　　*　　　*

When the news from Busta trickled down to Lerwick Barbara's first thought was for her son. 'Now that old eagle-woman will have sole charge of his destiny. How am I to bear it?' she asked her aunts. 'What will happen now?'

'Nothing will happen. Nothing will change,' Aunt Mary said firmly. 'She will continue to bring him up in the way to which she has accustomed him.'

'And,' Aunt Ellice said, 'it will be a long time before he marries, so Lady Busta will continue to reign supreme. She has been very cunning.'

'And very cruel,' Aunt Mary agreed. 'But never forget, Barbara, that old sins always come back to haunt people. She will suffer for them, yet.'

The following Christmas Barbara was sent her usual payments from Busta along with an even briefer note from Lady Elizabeth. As a result she felt sick and stifled that dark night. When she looked out of the window on to Commercial Street the snow was on the ground. Frost coating it was sparkling and flashing. She put on her outside shawl.

'You're never going out on a night like this, Barbara,' Aunt Ellice protested. 'You'll get your death of cold.'

'Let her go, Ellice,' Aunt Mary said. 'The fresh air will help her to sleep, and perhaps to eat a little better tomorrow. You won't be long dear?'

It wasn't far to walk down through one of the little lanes on to the sea front and over to the flat rock, her favourite place. At the edge of the sea there was no snow and no ice, only the black shining waves, and she didn't have long to wait until the white heads of her friends bobbed up out of the water.

After all these years of visiting them, and after all that Fisk had explained to her, Barbara fancied that she could understand what their strange sounds meant. She understood that the seals regarded the largest one as their king, and he made himself her special friend. She had no hesitation in telling him her thoughts. She was convinced that he understood every word that she said, a conviction that gave her immense strength.

On the way back up to 97 Commercial Street she thought that anyone seeing her or listening to her must think she was mad, and sometimes she wondered about the state of her mind after so many years of worry. For a few dubious, stolen hours with John Gifford she had certainly paid a heavy price.

She fretted, and fretted. Her fretting started up a pain in her lower stomach, a dull ache which made eating almost impossible. She fretted herself away to a shadow, so that the aunts sent a message to Mistress Lowrie Irvine at Symbister, Whalsay, and down at the boats managed to find another Whalsay boat whose skipper promised to deliver it.

Alice, dearest Niece.

We are very worried about your sister's state of health and would value your opinion. Above all, do not alarm Barbara by arriving here suddenly, but only send a message that you will be to see her the next time Lowrie runs down to Lerwick in his boat. We hope that you can arrange this at your earliest convenience.

Your loving Aunts, Mary and Ellice Bruce.

*　　　*　　　*

By now, it was a great relief to Barbara to lie down in her room in the afternoons when the pain was very bad. In such a way she hoped to disguise from her aunts how much she was suffering in the worst bouts of it, and it was only now and then that she could manage her walks down to the sea.

Lowrie Irvine took his wife, two toddlers and their baby down to Lerwick the very next day.

242

'Oh, you look so pretty, Alice,' Barbara smiled. 'Pretty, and happy.'

'Happy, yes,' Alice replied, while the aunts took charge of her children and cooed over them. 'Pretty, I never was. You were the pretty one, Barbara. What's happened to you? Are you ill?'

Alice couldn't believe her eyes. She tried her best to disguise the shock of seeing her sister so thin, almost emaciated, but with a large distended stomach.

'It's only a pain,' Barbara cringed. 'Down here. I've never really felt well since Gideon was born. As you know, Lady Elizabeth delivered him, and at the same time my marriage certificate disappeared for ever. I had it hidden in my pillow, but it vanished in a cloud of feathers. I couldn't prove Gideon was legitimate as a result, and that gave the Giffords the perfect excuse to adopt him. I haven't seen him since he was nearly seven years old.'

'That awful woman did all that to you, dearest sister?' Alice went over to the window-seat where they used to sit together in the old days watching for their father, George Pitcairn, trying to hide her tears. Suddenly she jumped up.

'Barbara!' she said, drying her eyes. 'It's the Busta coach! It's stopped along Commercial Street, and such a handsome young man is getting out of it!'

'Gideon,' Barbara breathed. 'Help me downstairs, Alice.'

But was it Gideon? The young man's eyes bore no resemblance to those little eyes that had looked up at her for almost seven years. He was very handsome, tall and fair with a pleasant open face; but he showed no sign of recognition.

'Gideon,' Barbara whispered with her heart beating like a drum, when he drew alongside them.

'Good morning, madam,' he smiled, doffed his hat and marched on.

'Oh, Alice,' Barbara said, her lips bloodless, 'after all this time of waiting *that* wasn't Gideon. What happened to my baby? Where has he gone?'

*   *   *

'You were quite right, dear Aunts,' Alice said at the door when she left. 'There's something far wrong with Barbara. I think she's in much greater pain that she's letting on. You must send for the apothecary to give her some medicine to ease it.'

'The apothecary . . .' they whispered. Nobody ever sent for Mr Fairfax unless their time had come.

Mr Fairfax came, took one look at Barbara and left a bottle, along with strict instructions.

'Three drops every four hours, and three

drops only. Do you have a pipette? No? Then here's one. I'll add it to the bill.'

The medicine didn't work for very long, they told Mr Fairfax. Perhaps a larger dose, to ease the poor girl?

'A teaspoonful every four hours, then. No more.'

That went on for a few weeks, but the pain was winning again.

'I cannot allow the dose more than every three hours,' Mr Fairfax told the Aunts. 'More than that would kill her.'

Aunt Mary and Aunt Ellice went early to bed these days, taking it in turn to administer Barbara's medicine. One of them must have slept in, that night in May when Barbara woke up, in an absolute hell of agony.

She thought of the pain in colours, every one of them harsh. There was the warning blue one, the hard, hard emerald, the violent purple, the ghastly black—but this one was the red one, the cruellest of all.

And the medicine was on the bedside table. They must have taken away the spoon to wash it. In desperation Barbara took out the cork, upended the bottle and drank the rest of its contents.

CHAPTER TWENTY

Almost immediately the pain went completely away. Without another thought, Barbara flung her shawl around her shoulders and tiptoed out of the house in her bare feet. She simply had to see her friends after all this time. She had to say goodbye before it was too late, for she knew what was coming.

She got half-way down the lane leading to the sea front before she collapsed under a gigantic onslaught of scarlet, fiery pain, far worse than any she had endured so far. But, although she couldn't walk, she crawled on her hands and knees to the flat rock, and all she could do there was curl herself up and try to protect herself from the agony.

She thought of Gideon. She thought of her whole life. It all flashed before her in a few minutes while the water lapped around her and soaked her. Just for an instant she thought it was cooling her, but she was mistaken. The pain came rushing back again.

And then, when she knew she could stand no more, the torture of a slow, agonising death began to gather strength in the same way as a huge roller far out on the ocean harnesses all its brute force to come nearer and nearer and then to strike.

It was coming, it was coming, a blazing

fireball of pain. Barbara looked towards the sea for deliverance, and straight into the eyes of John Fisken, her beloved Fisk.

*　　　*　　　*

Fisk eased her gently off the flat rock and swam her down into the sea. Above their heads a huge wave, scarlet and vicious and screaming, roared past. Down, down they went to the bottom of the sea and into a vast white and silver cave, a cathedral of arches and altars and magnificent rock sculptures, all of them mother-of-pearl, where the waves beating on the walls made music soaring to the roof like the sound of an organ playing. He laid her down on a wide ledge where her tired body sank into soft sea grasses and she slept at last. She woke up when feathery hands were stroking her and, looking down at her body, Barbara saw that the hands were covering her with tiny scales of mother-of-pearl, dressing her for a different life in palest opalescent pinks and lemons and blues and lilacs from her waist right down to her tail.

'You're a mermaid now,' one of her ladies told her. 'You can be a mermaid, the same as we are, any time you like. But one day you will be a queen, the Queen of the White Seals.'

They held up a mirror and she saw that she was young again and full of life and fun. She laughed and whisked her tail to see what it was like and then she was off, diving and swimming exultantly in the crystal waters until Fisk caught up with her. Gradually, he helped her to change into a white seal and they swam off together to the Grind of Navir, and into the Red Palace under the Holes of Scraada—just around the corner of the coast from Busta, where they could always hear The Call.

As Fisk's wife Barbara knew true happiness for the first time. Her earthly shackles fell away from her altogether. When her pups were born she had almost forgotten the world she lived in before, except for a strange sort of eagle they used to call Lady Elizabeth.

And, of course, Gideon.

*   *   *

They found Barbara Pitcairn's earthly remains on a flat rock down by the sea. At first they thought it was only a bundle of sodden old rags, until they turned it around and her dead eyes stared up at them.

The news of this discovery reached Busta House before nightfall. Early next morning Lady Busta appeared at 97 Commercial Street in Lerwick.

'A funeral costs moncy,' she told the sorrowing, stunned Aunts in superior tones, with a glacial stare. 'I will attend to everything.'

'Perhaps she means to be kind,' Aunt Ellice said tearfully.

'That woman? Kind?' Aunt Mary was not so sure.

A week later they went to view the grave in the company of Alice and Lowrie Irvine, down from Whalsay now that the gravestone had been erected, sure that Lady Busta would have seen to it properly.

They couldn't believe their eyes when they read the inscription.

'The final insult . . .' Aunt Mary Bruce whispered.

> 'Barbara Pitcairn
> Spinster of this Parish,
> 1730–1765

'No, Lady Busta wasn't kind,' Aunt Ellice sobbed.

'Kind?' Lowrie exploded. 'By Christ, the old bitch was bitter right to the end.'

Alice and her two aunts laid down their flowers on the grave in floods of tears. On the way back to Whalsay Alice was still weeping, with her head on her husband's shoulder.

'Oh, Lowrie, it isn't right.'

'It's a bloody disgrace, and everyone who sees it for the rest of time will say the same. Come, Alice,' he said when they docked, 'we'll go home to bed.'

That night their fourth child was conceived.

'What shall we call her?' Lowrie asked when this latest daughter was born.

'Barbara—what else? Barbara Pitcairn, in her memory.'

We hope you have enjoyed this Large Print book. Other Chivers Press or Thorndike Press Large Print books are available at your library or directly from the publishers.

For more information about current and forthcoming titles, please call or write, without obligation, to:

Chivers Press Limited
Windsor Bridge Road
Bath BA2 3AX
England
Tel. (01225) 335336

OR

Thorndike Press
P.O. Box 159
Thorndike, Maine 04986
USA
Tel. (800) 223-2336

All our Large Print titles are designed for easy reading, and all our books are made to last.